Cassie

by
John McAulay

Kilcoy
2016

CASSIE

First published in Australia in 2017
by John McAulay
Kilcoy, Queensland

© John McAulay 2017

ISBN: 978-0-646-96572-7

Also by John McAulay

Pass the Ball
Aussie Yarns
Reminiscence

CHAPTER ONE

His eyes never left the girl as she fidgeted nervously on the foot-path across the street. She moved from one foot to the other and glanced to left and right every few seconds. Occasionally she walked a few metres, paused, and then returned to her spot in front of the jewellery shop window. Its brightly lit display silhou-etted her frail figure dressed in a skimpy black skirt topped by a flowery blouse, unbuttoned at the throat further than it should have been. Not that it revealed anything of interest he thought to himself, letting his gaze wander down to her chest, her thin hips and spindly legs.

His gaze returned to her face. The face of a child, he decided, in spite of the heavy make-up. Even at the distance that separated them he was sure he could detect apprehension, maybe fear in her eyes. Her actions alone demonstrated a lack of confidence that could only be born of fear, but what was she afraid of? And what was she doing hanging around the street on her own? She was obviously in trouble. He wondered why.

"You no like sir?"

The voice behind his shoulder startled him, and he turned to see a waitress indicating the plate full of scarcely touched chick-en chow mien in front of him. He smiled at her, and taking up his chop-sticks, he popped a piece of chicken into his mouth.

"No, it's fine Suzy thank you. I was just dreaming."

Nodding and bowing, she withdrew, leaving him to once again turn his attention across the street. She was gone. Reaching over, he parted the bead curtain beside him to widen his view. She had moved a few metres along and was looking at the restaurant. Attracted by the movement of the curtain, her eyes flickered in his direction. He let the beads drop from his hand and returned briefly to his meal. Maybe it was none of his business. Perhaps he shouldn't be concerned with other people's troubles. After all, he had enough of his own.

But he couldn't help himself. Glancing up again, he saw that she had returned to her position in front of the window, but now she was not alone. His view of her was now partly obscured by a young man. They seemed to be chatting quite happily, and when she moved slightly, he saw with relief that she was smiling. But there was something about the young man that worried him. Too young to be her father and much too old to be a friend. There was something else too. Was that just arrogance in his stance and manner he detected, or worse, aggression? He didn't like the look of him at all. Once again his chopsticks lay idle in his fingers as he stared transfixed at the tableau across the street.

Her fidgeting had resulted in them now being in profile and he noticed that the smile had vanished, and now he thought her expression showed dread, even terror. Her body language and look on her face made the hairs rise on the back of his neck. If only he could hear what they were saying.

Then the young man took her hand and started to lead her away. Suddenly she stopped, pulled her hand away, and, with a shake of her head, started to walk quickly back in the opposite direction. He followed her, and grasping her shoulder, spun her round to face him. By now she was quite obviously distraught, and pulling away, she darted across the street, straight in his direction.

His chair scraped on the tiles as he rose quickly to his feet.

Throwing some cash on the table to cover the bill, he walked quickly towards the door, his mind made up. Feeling concern was one thing, but now it was time to take action.

❦

Cassie stared sightlessly out of the window of the Greyhound bus as it wound its way down the Toowoomba range towards Brisbane. A steady drizzle of rain drifted in streaks across the glass, blurring her view of the dreary mountainside scenery, prompting what should have been despondency and dejection. But not today. Today she was excited, ecstatic even. She had done it. After weeks of planning, she had taken the plunge. At last she was free to do as she pleased. She hardly dared to imagine what lay ahead of her, but surely it would be better than what her life had become. Even the sensation of her tea-shirt, jeans and joggers felt good after being forced to wear that stupid school uniform since she started boarding at the beginning of the year. Not only a daggy dress, but black school shoes and stockings no less, and topped off by that silly little preppy hat. A self satisfied smile spread across her face as she thought of some cleaner at the bus terminal finding it all stuffed in a rubbish bin. Already she felt like a new person, an adult person, no less.

She searched in her bag for her compact, flicked it open, and surveyed the image that stared back at her from the mirror. Red hair and freckles she thought somewhat disgustedly. Well not red exactly. More auburn actually. She turned her head from side to side, pulled her hair to one side, then piled it experimentally on top. Perhaps she should get it cut short, even dyed brunette, or permed maybe. The thought made her smile into the mirror. Ugh! Too thin-lipped she decided. Once again she rummaged in her bag and produced a bright red lip-stick she had snitched from her mother's dressing table weeks ago. Steadying herself against the movements of the bus she carefully applied it and then surveyed her work. Marvellous! She looked years older already, she decided, and prettier. Just wait till she could get a haircut and some decent clothes. Looking out the window as they swung onto the overpass at Helidon she was pleased to see that the rain had stopped.

Clothes. Haircuts. Money, she thought. How was she going to survive? Expo 88 was happening, making things dearer than usual no doubt with all the thousands of extra visitors. Still, it might make losing herself in the city a bit easier, just in case anyone came looking for her. Glancing around to make sure no-one was watching she extracted her purse from her bag. She counted the notes, carefully saved from pocket money and birthday gifts just in case this occasion ever arrived. Well now it had. After paying her bus fare she was left with one hundred and fifteen dollars. Not much for someone starting out on a new life she thought wryly. She would have to get a job pretty quickly, that was for sure. She packed everything back in her bag and settled back in her seat, luxuriating in her new found feeling of independence and maturity.

Thank heavens for good old Dad, she thought. He'd sent her fifty dollars for her birthday and that had made all the difference to her decision to do a runner. If only he knew. She still loved her dad, even though she had seen him only a few times over the last five years. She missed him, and the life-style on the farm she had enjoyed until she was ten. She shut her eyes to hide the tears that welled to them at the memories that came flooding back to her.

❧

"Help me Cam," she squealed. "I can't hold on."

"Yes you can. I'm coming."

Her brother slithered down the bank towards where she was battling valiantly to hold onto a rod that was whipping from side to side as something under the murky water struggled to free itself. Cassie's frail six year old body was jerking around and her face was flushed as she fought to keep her balance.

"Hurry up!" she screamed as her feet reached the water's edge. But Cameron arrived too late. With a final effort by her catch, the rod was wrenched from her fingers and sailed off down the river, while she stumbled and fell into the shallows.

"Now look what you've done," she said, dragging herself crying and dripping wet up the bank. "Wait till I tell Mum."

"What I've done?" he yelled at her. "How about you? I leave you to mind my rod for a few minutes and you've gone and lost it. And probably the biggest fish I've ever caught. God you're weak."

Cassie smiled to herself as the memory of her brother's frustration came back to her. Served him right she decided. He was three years older than her but treated her more like a twin brother, involving her in all his exploits on the farm almost since she could walk. What fond memories she had of that time.

Their farm was a grain property owned by her grandfather. Her father had left school at fourteen and worked on the place ever since. He grew into a man of simple tastes, totally dedicated to his profession, and to his aging parents. Those tasks may have remained the only elements in his life had he not met a pretty young teacher who was posted to the local two teacher school just down the road. At thirty, he was ten years her senior, and became besotted with her.

Angela Rowland was a city girl who had never been west of Toowoomba before the Education Department sent her to what she regarded as the ends of the earth. At first she hated her new life with a passion, but as the tall young farmer exerted his charms on her, she became attracted to some aspects of rural life, including him. But it was when she paid her first visit to meet his parents that he won her over. She fell in love with the homestead. It was a magnificent old weatherboard house built at the turn of the century. It was set low to the ground, had wide verandas on three sides, and nestled comfortably on a rise overlooking the river. An avenue of Jacarandas led up to a garden highlighted by a magnificent rose garden. Mrs Douglas had furnished and deco-rated the large airy rooms tastefully and young Angela had vi-sions of herself comfortably ensconced in the position of mistress of this very desirable domain.

Unfortunately, her future husband omitted to tell her that his parents had no immediate plans of moving, and when they were married after a short courtship, they moved into the much less sa-lubrious accommodation provided by an old manager's cottage. To her ongoing frustration, that is where they stayed for the birth of Cameron and Cassandra, and indeed for her whole time on the property, while Bill's parents continued to enjoy the comforts of the homestead.

One day all this will be ours, he used to tell her. We'll move into the big house, and when he gets older Cam can live here in this house. Not if I can help it, Angela had thought. All her grand dreams of a luxurious life as the wife of a wealthy property owner and respected member of the local squattocracy had disappeared over the years as she was forced to face the reality of life on the land. It left her bitter and resentful, her only joy being her children, for whom she had grander plans.

Her frustration was never directed at them. She adored them, showering them with affection spoiling them shamelessly, especially Cameron, who she thought could do no wrong. Their childhood was idyllic as they roamed the property on their ponies, built cubby houses and played and fished at the nearby river. They were wild spirits enjoying the pleasures of a simple country life.

The one concession their mother did wring from their farm obsessed father was an annual holiday with her parents at the Gold Coast. Three weeks each year of enjoying a different kind of lifestyle, one of shops, movies, and fun parks, and of pigging out on takeaways.

Cassie recalled it all vividly, especially the fact that more often than not they had to travel down by train as their father was too involved in some urgent work on the farm to waste his time sitting on hot sand on some salty beach as he so elegantly used to put it. Thinking back, she didn't think there was much love lost between him and his in-laws either. Bill Douglas thought Angela's mother was a spendthrift socialite, while her father drank too much and was not over impressed with his tomboy grandchildren.

While it hadn't occurred to her at the time, Cassie now recalled the wistfulness on her mother's face as they headed back out west. She would sit in silence as they left the coast and the mountains behind and approached another year on the flat, expressionless, boring, and yes, shopless plains around Roma. Little wonder that their family would be torn apart down the track.

The stresses made it inevitable, only awaiting the circumstances that would prove insurmountable for her parents.

⁂

Cassie pulled herself up in her seat and blinked as she looked out the window. Bright sunshine now streamed through the broken clouds, dispelling the thoughts of her parent's difficulties, and lifting her spirits. They had reached the beautiful Lockyer Valley, with its meticulously laid out farms growing all sorts of vegetables. Row after row of cabbages, lettuces, carrots and potatoes stretched into the distance. Water rained down on them from miles of irrigation pipes in some fields, while in others, pickers laboured in teams to harvest the crops for market. She was still a country girl at heart, and the sight always filled her with a pleasant feeling of well-being.

She looked at her watch and wondered if anyone had noticed her missing from school. Probably not yet, she decided, having taken the precaution of getting a pass to go shopping after school. A smug smile hung on her lips as she thought of the mayhem it would cause when they did realise she wasn't back on time. All hell would break loose as they tried to track her movements and find her before they had to report her absence to her mother and eventually even the police. With a bit of luck, by the time they did, she would be well away and lost amongst the teeming crowds in Brisbane.

Serves them right, she decided. They were part of the reason for her decision. Not the teachers. She got on okay with them, but not so most of her fellow boarders. Stuck up bitches! No wonder her mother had insisted she should go there. It was just a status symbol to her. She was a social snob, simple as that. Insisted

8

on calling her Cassandra in recent times, even though she knew hated it. Cassie had been good enough in the old days out on the farm, but not now. She put on airs and graces well above her station in life and expected Cassie to follow her example. Not in this life she thought.

Obviously it suited her mother very well to be able to boast to her friends that "Cassandra boards at Fairholme you know. Such a lovely school." She could see her saying it, wine glass in hand at some gallery opening or book launch with her new found acquaintances. All spin, when the real reason Cassie was there was to keep her well out of the way so Angela could enjoy her new life unhindered by a schoolgirl living with her. More time for Aldo. With a shudder, she drew her thoughts back to the school.

Perhaps it had been her fault. From day one she had a chip on her shoulder. Pulled as she had been from a reasonably happy school life at the Coast and dropped into a group of girls who had been living together for years, what would you expect. Instant friendships? Not likely, not with that snooty bunch. Oh she had tried at the start, but they seemed to look on her as an interloper, intent on busting up their long-standing friendships. She wasn't exactly ostracised, just not included, and over time she became considered a loner who shunned inclusion. Well good luck to them, she thought. They won't have to put up with me any more.

༞

What had really set her off was Parent's Day. Before that, she could put up with the social exclusion of the other girls, but that became impossible after the visit from her mother and her newest boyfriend, Aldo Mercini. The embarrassment they caused her was just altogether too much. They had roared up in Aldo's open top Mercedes, parked in a teacher's reserved car-park, and came swanning around the school arm in arm like two film stars. Angela wore a tight mini-skirt, knee length boots and a floppy bright yellow hat, while Aldo looked like the spiv he probably was with an open necked shirt and gold chain. How gross! "Yoo hoo, Cassandra," she had called across the quadrangle. "We're here. Come and say hello to Aldo."

⅍

The following days were hell.

"Ooh Cassandra," they had teased. "She's sooo hot! And just look at the toy-boy she's caught. He's gorgeous, and sooo rich. What a cougar!"

Cassie was mortified, and decided the time had come to put into action a plan that had been in her mind for weeks. Maybe a call from the school advising of her disappearance would bring her mother to her senses. Then again, apart from the social stigma of being the mother of a run-away daughter, she might be pleased to be rid of her. More time for Mr. Wonderful.

⅍

As the bus joined the throng of vehicles streaming along Ipswich Road, Cassie's thoughts returned to her father. Poor old Dad. He didn't deserve the hand fate had dealt him. It wasn't his fault that he married the wrong woman. He did his best to keep Angela happy and well provided for, but he couldn't give her the life she so obviously craved. In the end, Cassie thought he was probably pretty comfortable with his new solitary life, working the farm and living quite contentedly in the cottage.

10

He had always been pleased to have her and Cameron on their rare holiday visits, and snuck her extra cash from time to time. But he seldom wrote to me, she recalled, and seemed totally disinterested in how she was going at school, or at home for that matter. Maybe he thought he was well out of it too, leaving him to concentrate totally on the farm and looking after his now ageing parents.

Cassie had briefly harboured the idea of heading west when she ran away, throwing herself on him, and begging to be allowed to stay, but on reflection, decided it wouldn't work. For a start, he couldn't look after a teenage schoolgirl, and secondly, he would probably be forced to return her to her mother anyway, as she was legal guardian of Cassie and her brother, although now eighteen, Cam was free to lead his own life. Lucky him, she thought. Lucky me too. I've joined him.

⁊

As the bus continued its steady crawl towards the city, she recalled the day her happy childhood had been torn apart. She had been ten years old on that fateful day when they left Dad to his farm.

How excited she had been that morning. She had made the athletics team to compete in the district sports in Dalby. Her brother was taking a day off school, and the whole family was going to watch her compete. As she was putting on her sports uniform, a discussion in the kitchen between her parents degenerated into a rowdy argument. She listened at her bedroom door.

"You can't be serious," her mother had shouted. "Not today. Haven't you seen how excited she is? You've just got to come with us."

"I've said I'm sorry," he yelled back. "I'll explain to Cassie. She'll understand better than you that the farm's more important than a bloody sports day."

"Well if that's your attitude, why did you agree to go in the first place?"

"Because, you silly woman, until I heard the weather forecast this morning I didn't know there was rain on the way."

"The bloody farm," her mother spat at him. "The all important, all consuming bloody farm. I'm sick of it!"

He lowered his voice to a growl that Cassie strained to hear. "Well I'm not, and I've got three hundred acres of wheat to plant before dark, so that's what I'm going to do. I'll talk to Cassie on the way." Probably he was too upset, but for whatever reason he never did. He simply stomped out the door in a huff, while Cassie watched through her window with tears in her eyes as he disappeared into the shed.

Her mother came up behind and put her arms around her. "I'm sorry Cassie. I did my best, but you know him. Here," she said, handing her a handkerchief. "Dry your eyes and come and have some breakfast. There's something I want to tell you and Cameron."

So that was how Cassie's life fell apart. Her mother told them she had been planning on leaving for some time, and today's confrontation was the last straw. Maybe he would come to his senses if she showed him she was serious. He'd probably be begging forgiveness in no time, and then they could all come home.

After watching the tractor and planter head away from the shed, they spent a couple of hours packing as much of their belongings as they could fit in the station wagon. Then, after leaving a note on the kitchen table, they drove out of their father's life. Forever, Cassie thought. There was no way her mother would ever go back there.

⁂

The bus turned off Roma Street and entered the Transport Terminal. She pulled herself up in her seat, squared her shoulders, and grimly looked the future in the face. No point now in pining for the past or pondering what might have been. Here she was to all intents and purposes all alone in the world, and the sooner she got started on her new life the better. She gathered up her bag and joined the string of passengers heading for the door.

CHAPTER TWO

Cassie looked around nervously as she stepped from the bus, half expecting to see someone from the school waiting to drag her back. That's a bit silly she thought to herself. They probably still hadn't realised she was missing, let alone had time to track her to the bus and reach Brisbane in time to intercept her. Still, the sooner she was clear of this last connection to Toowoomba the better. She collected her backpack from the luggage compartment and hurried away.

Where to next, she wondered? Diesel fumes and dust mixed with the body odours of travel weary passengers combined to make the atmosphere of the cavernous interior of the terminal stifling. After the quiet calm of the trip, she now found herself somewhat overwhelmed and disconcerted by the noise of vehicles arriving and leaving, the strident instructions coming from the P.A. system, and the laughter and chatter of the throngs around her. The sooner she was out of here the better. Hoisting the backpack that now contained all of her worldly possessions, she joined the surge heading for the central court.

The peals of the City Hall clock announcing 5 o'clock reminded her that the day was running out. It would be dark in a couple of hours and she needed to find somewhere to spend the night before then. She suddenly realised this was a subject to which she hadn't given much thought, but now, with her limited funds in mind, she wondered just what her next step should be. God, she didn't want to spend a night on the streets.

Don't panic, she told herself. Think. A McDonalds sign

caught her eye and she realised she was hungry and thirsty too. Might as well grab something here while it's handy she thought. With a Big Mac and a coke in front of her she settled herself at a table and looked around the other customers, many of whom seemed much like herself, if a little older. Casually dressed and sporting backpacks, they were obviously young travellers out to see the world. Foot-loose and fancy-free, she thought. Just like me. She wondered where they stayed and how they went about finding work and decided this might be a good place to start her education on how to survive in her new life.

As she watched she noticed that they all seemed to head in the same direction as they left the food court. She decided to follow them and found them gathered in an area that seemed to cater for backpackers. Squeezing her way through them she came to a large notice board. It contained many listings for cheap accommodation in and around the city, and others offering employment. Unfortunately, a quick browse showed that most jobs were in rural areas, and she wasn't about to leave the city just yet. First things first, she decided. Somewhere to stay tonight was top of the list. She scribbled down the addresses of several cheap hostels in the city and, hoisting her backpack, marched out into the street.

⚘

Her fellow travellers had beaten her to the punch. After an hour of searching the streets she had been unable to find a single vacancy, and once again she was viewing the prospect of spending the night on the street. One to go, she sighed, and that was in Fortitude Valley, a good half hour's walk away. She had heard bad things about The Valley, reputed to be the heart of all sorts of illegal activities, but with no better option she hurried off down Ann Street.

A voice behind her called out and she spun around.

"Hey Miss!"

It was a policeman motioning her to come to him. Her heart sank. For an instant the thought of making a run for it flashed through her mind. How had they found her so quickly? What would they do with her? Take her back to school, or straight to her mother? The thought of both alternatives horrified her. She tentatively walked towards him.

"Me sir?" she asked.

"Yes you miss," he replied, waiting at the street corner until she returned. "See that?" he asked, aiming his thumb at the traffic light beside him.

"Yes."

"Well how come you didn't see it when you just crossed against the red light? Dreaming about the boyfriend were you?"

The blood that had drained from her face suddenly returned and she found herself blushing. Is that all he wants? Thank God!

"No sir. I'm sorry. I must have missed it. But there wasn't any traffic coming," she added defensively.

The law officer eyed her severely. "That's beside the point," he said. "Crossing against the signal is still illegal." He started to remove his charge book from his pocket. Cassie stared at the footpath and said nothing. Then he put it back.

"Go on. Off you go," he said. "I must be getting soft, but don't try it again or it'll cost you a fine. Got me?"

"Yes sir. Thank you. I'm sorry. I won't do it again." Giving him a nervous smile, she turned and hurried away.

"You'd better not," he called after her, and then smiled to

himself as he thought of his own daughter who had probably got away with the same misdemeanour hundreds of times. I just hope the copper who catches her is as soft as me, he thought with a chuckle.

⁂

Darkness was starting to fill the streets of The Valley when Cassie found the address she had been seeking. Well, this is my last chance, she thought. Here's hoping. Her spirits rose as she reached the door. "Vacancies" the sign said. Tentatively she entered and fronted the counter in the foyer. Another sign taped to the wall said "Ring bell for service," so she did, and waited. After a minute or so, she rang again, just as a frumpy woman with a walking stick in one hand and a cigarette in the other hobbled out of a near-by room.

"Okay. Hold your horses," she said. "I'm comin' as quick as I can." She heaved herself onto a stool behind the counter. "Now, what can I do for you?"

"Do you have a room available please?"

"A room? No rooms here I'm afraid missy," she said with a chuckle. Cassie's heart sank. "But I got a bed, if you want one. This ain't no Hilton Hotel with rooms. It's a hostel, with dorms. Now do you want a bed or not?"

"How much?" Cassie asked.

"Twenty a night, or a hundred a week, paid up front of course," she said.

"Could I just pay for one night now and let you know tomorrow if I need to stay longer please?" Cassie asked, not quite sure if this place was the best she could find.

"Okay by me," her landlady said, "but no guarantees about

tomorra. First in best dressed around here is the rule. That'll be twenty bucks then," she said reaching under the counter and producing two grey looking white sheets and a pillowcase with in-ground stains where thousands of heads had left their mark.

⁂

My God Cassie thought. This is what I ran away from. Even worse, because the dormitory in which she now stood was strewn with bags and parcels and clothes and ....people, male and female, lounging around, chatting and laughing. Cigarette smoke hung around them, and although she wasn't sure, she imagined not all of it was legal either, which could explain their exuberance. Panic rose to her chest. How can I ever survive in here she wondered.

She searched the line of beds for an unoccupied one and was relieved to find one in a far corner of the room. She dropped the linen she had been issued onto the bare mattress beside the battered looking blue blankets and slung her backpack underneath. She sat tentatively on the edge and heaved a sigh, the deep breath of fetid air causing her to cough and splutter. The two girls a few beds down glanced at her and smiled.

"Want a drag?" one said, proffering a reefer in her direction. "It'll fix that cough you've got." They both giggled.

"No thanks.," she said. "I've got to go out." She stumbled towards the door, trying not to breath deeply on the way.

⁂

Bewildered and crestfallen she wandered through the sleazy back streets on her way back to the hostel. For three days she had walked from one end of the city to the other, asking for work at every shop and business she passed, but to no avail. A few cafes had let her work off a meal by washing dishes, but she needed a

18

proper job, and she needed it now. Her money was running out fast.

On the first day she had noticed a Government Employment Office and had entered eagerly, assuming they would have heaps of jobs available. They probably did, but first you had to register and fill in the paper work. She couldn't bring herself to do it. Name, age, address, next of kin, experience, last job. The questions were all too hard, and she assumed, could lead to her being easily traced by anyone looking for her. Maybe tomorrow she would have more luck.

Lying sleepless in bed that night, listening to the muffled snuffling and snoring around her, she considered her options. Unless something turned up tomorrow, this would probably be her last night in a bed. Hunger would force her to spend her last few dollars on food, and the hostel ruled out even asking for credit. She had already been looking around public areas for somewhere to sleep if it came to that. Brunswick Street railway station looked like the best bet. At least it had toilets and was well lit, but she didn't fancy the thought of hiding out there on her own overnight. Please God don't let it come to that she prayed in the dark. Suddenly all of the sleeping strangers around her seemed like best friends. At least they made her feel safe.

❧

Tears welled to her eyes as she trudged back to the hostel after another fruitless day of job seeking. Still nothing more than a promise of maybe next week from a Greek cafe in Queen Street, but she couldn't wait till then. Desperation turned her mind to surrender. She could ring her mother and undoubtedly be sent back to school where she would be laughed at and teased even worse than before. Whatever else, she was not going to do that. She could call on her father for help she supposed, but there was no certainty that he would agree with what she had done, and would tell her mother anyway. No, that was out too. There were probably some charities that would give her a bed, but they would more than likely check with the police to see if she was a missing person, which she certainly would be by now. No, she decided, somehow she had to make a go of it. The alternatives were just too awful to consider.

A flashing red "DONT WALK" sign brought her to a halt. I'm not going to risk that again, she thought, searching nervously around for a policeman. As she waited for it to change her attention was drawn to the opposite corner of the intersection. A girl whom she had noticed several times around the place stood there talking to a man who Cassie judged must be twice her age. He was old enough to be her father, but was quite obviously not. Surely not, she said under her breath. She's not much older than me. Naive she might be but Cassie's mother had warned her about The Valley, the City's centre for night-life, and consequently drugs and prostitution. Surely not, she said under her breath, but I wish I could hear what they're saying. Cassie watched as the girl leaned back against the wall and smiled at him seductively. Just as the light changed to green, she took his hand and led him off down the street.

Later on in her life she would wonder from time to time just what made her decide to follow them, drawn like a moth to a flame. Somewhere in everyone's life they experience a life changing decision which has a monumental impact on the rest of their lives. This was hers. She hurried across the street.

Her nose twitched as she shadowed them down a poorly lit back street. Urine and garbage smells hung in the still night air. The occasional person she passed seemed to be intent on escaping the place as fast as possible, and she could certainly understand why. There was an air of malevolence and desolation which made her shiver. She wondered what the drab buildings lining the street contained as she scanned their blank windows. Offices? Factories? Surely not houses?

When she looked back, they had disappeared. Feeling rather guilty for spying on them, she crept along the footpath until she came to the building they must have entered. Similar to all the others, it was two stories of solid dark brick, with uniform rectangular windows on both levels. Lights burned in some of them, including the ones on either side of a single solid door.

As she paused, unsure what to do, she heard muffled voices. How strange, she thought. It must be a house of some kind. Then she noticed a faded sign above the door.

HARMONY APARTMENTS
ROOMS TO LET
APPLY WITHIN

Yair, if only, Cassie thought. Even this decrepit dump would probably be a safe haven if she had some money, but she didn't. With a sigh, she turned to retrace her steps, and then she saw it. Her heart missed a beat. Stuck to the wall with sticky tape was another sign, one she had been seeking for days. Well hardly a sign actually. Just a notice really, scratched on a piece of cardboard in felt pen it read...

WANTED
DOMESTIC HELP

At last! She paused for a second or two to glance once more around the sleazy surroundings. It was hardly the kind of place she would have chosen to work, but her hunger and thoughts of sleeping rough reminded her of the parsimonious situation in which she found herself. Setting aside her fears, she sucked in a deep breath, and with as much confidence as she could muster, she knocked on the heavy wooden door.

CHAPTER THREE

"It's not locked. Come on in," a gravely voice called from some-where inside the building.

Cassie turned the knob, pushed the door slightly open and cautiously peered around it. She saw that it opened into a foyer containing a green plastic covered sofa and a desk with a vase of artificial flowers on one end and a phone on the other. The floor was covered with a well-worn dark brown carpet, and the whole scene was rather dimly lit by a gaudily shaded light that hung from the centre of the ceiling. Steeling herself, she sucked in a deep breath, pushed inside and closed the door.

"Hello," she called in a tentative voice that almost caught in her throat. She coughed quietly to clear it and then asked in a louder voice, "Is anyone there?"

The gravely voice answered from along a passage-way that ran towards the back of the building. "Course there is. Who do you think answered you? A spook?" It was followed by a throaty laugh. "Come on down the hall sweetie. I'm a bit tied up at the moment."

Thank heavens for that Cassie thought as she tentatively edged her way along the hall. At least it's a woman. On her right the fee-ble light from the foyer allowed her to see into a large lounge room cluttered with a variety of over-stuffed chairs. In the gloom she saw a television flickering away in the far corner, and she felt the pres-ence of, rather than saw, a couple of people hidden in the chairs. Quickly averting her eyes she continued on towards a pool of light flooding out of an open door to the left at the end of the passage, passing as she went another door leading to what appeared to be a dining room containing a large table and many chairs.

"I'm in here sweetie," the voice called. "Don't be shy. I won't bite you." Again the throaty laugh.

The room she entered was a kitchen, the largest one Cassie had ever seen, except the one at school of course. A long bench ran through its middle, and various appliances and cupboards covered the walls, except for a window at the far end and a door which obviously led into the dining room. Florescent lights flooded the scene that presented itself, and there, in the middle of the room, with her hands embedded in a large steel bowl, stood the owner of the voice, and the laugh, which now gurgled forth again.

"Deary me missy, you look like you've seen a ghost," the owner of both gushed. "No need to be frightened. Come on in. I'm Mrs Jones, although most of them hereabouts call me Jonesy. Sorry I can't shake your hand," she said, holding up her own flour covered pair. "What can I do for you sweetie?"

Her friendliness caused Cassie to heave an inaudible sigh of relief as she moved forward to stand on the opposite side of the table. "Hello," she said in the strongest voice she could muster. "I'm Cassie. I've come about the job," mustering up the best smile her strained nerves would allow.

Freda Jones dumped the dough onto the bench-top and took up a rolling pin. "Well you're just in time then aren't you?" she cackled. "As you can see, I could use another pair of hands. How about fetching that pie dish over there for me please Cassie?"

Cassie retrieved the large dish full of mince that sat cooling on the bench near the window and placed it with-in reach of the lady she now knew to be Mrs Jones whose appearance matched her voice to perfection. She was rather plump, with a happy round face topped by a mop of wild looking black hair. Dressed in a simple dress which was almost covered by a large food stained apron, Cassie smiled to herself at the thought of how different this woman was from her prim and proper mother. No short skirts and high boots for this lady she decided.

"Thanks dearie," Mrs Jones said as she threw the pastry over the pie dish and started to press it down around the edges. "Do you mind if I get this in the oven first? Then we can have a nice cup of tea and talk business eh?" She trimmed the excess off around the edge, prodded a few holes in the top, and put it into the wall oven behind her. Then, turning back to Cassie, she wiped her hands on her apron, and with a broad smile and a nod in the direction of an electric kettle on a side bench, she answered her own question. "I'll just pop the kettle on and you can tell me why a young girl like you wants a job in a place like this," she said, her shrewd eyes taking in the apprehensive young girl waiting patiently. "Just go through to the dining room and I'll be there in a jiffy. The light switch is on the right hand side."

"There we are," Mrs Jones said as she set a tray on the end of the table. I thought you might like to help me get rid of some of this," she said laying a plate with a large slice of chocolate cake on it in front of Cassie. "It's the last thing someone like me should be eating," she added with laugh, patting her ample stomach. Then, settling herself in the chair at the end of the table, she filled both their cups, added milk, took a huge gulp and then leant back and appraised the young girl who was nervously nibbling on her cake.

"So tell me Cassie," she said in a friendly tone, "What brings you to my door looking for a job? If you don't mind my saying so, you look like you should be at school rather than washing dishes for me. Run away from home have you?"

Cassie almost choked on her cake. She was shocked at the woman's perceptiveness. "How did you know?" she almost whispered, putting down the cake and averting her eyes.

Mrs Jones gave one of her throaty chuckles. "Oh don't be so surprised," she said. "You're not the first run-away to come through my door you know, and I'll bet you're not the last. Maybe it's because I did the same thing myself many years ago eh? Now, eat up and tell me about it."

Shrewd eyes watched her over the rim of the cup. "I just couldn't take it any more Mrs Jones." Cassie paused, and seeing what she felt was genuine understanding and compassion on the woman's face, she rushed on. "It's a long story, but I'm almost sorry I did it now. I've no money left and haven't been able to find any work, and now I've got nowhere to live either. Please give me a chance at this job. I'll do anything, and I won't ask for much pay." Again she paused waiting for an answer, and then in panic asked "It is still available isn't it?"

Mrs Jones reached across the table and took the hands that had been wringing nervously in front of her. For once the cheerful expression had left her face and she was deadly serious as she said, "Of course it is, and it's yours if you want it. I've helped lots of girls like you over the years. Some of them became like daughters to me, they did." A dreamy look came over her face.

"Never had any kids of my own you know. Apparently Mr Jones was firing blanks all the years we were married, and by the time I ditched him, I was too old to start with a new man." This time the infectious cackle held a note of suppressed sadness.

This broke the tension and she was pleased at the smile it

26

brought to Cassie's lips. "Come on then," she said. "Eat up and then I'll show you around. I think we can probably find somewhere for you to stay too, although all the rooms are taken at the moment. Would you mind sharing?"

"Not at all," she replied. "Not after boarding school and a few days in a back-packer's hostel with twenty others, males and females I might add. And, unisex bathrooms too," she added as an afterthought.

"Well you'll be pleased to hear there's none of that here," Mrs Jones said. "All my rooms are let to girls. I think Angie might be willing to share with you till a room becomes available. Shouldn't take long. There's always someone moving on."

She led Cassie through the communal rooms on the ground floor and introduced her to the three girls watching T V. Her own quarters took up one corner of the rest. Upstairs consisted of a long passage with five bedrooms on each side and a bathroom and laundry at the far end. The place was drab, but clean, and the residents had all created signs for their doors with their names drawn with varying degrees of artistic ability. First names only Cassie noticed.

Back in the kitchen, she hurried to take the pie from the oven. Cassie's stomach ached at the aroma it gave off, and her new boss noticed the hunger in her eyes.

"How soon can you fetch your gear from the hostel Cas? I don't imagine it will take long to pack eh?" she joked. "Probably best if you do that first and I'll have tea ready when you get back. Angie should be home by then too."

"I'll run all the way," Cassie said. "Twenty minutes tops." She was already heading for the door as she heard that friendly cackle behind her.

❧

With a large helping of pie and vegetables and a bowl of tinned fruit and ice-cream inside her Cassie felt full for the first time in days. She hurried to help Mrs Jones clear the dishes from the table and stack them near the sink. Six of the residents had turned up for the meal, but Angie was not amongst them. Nor, she noticed, was the girl she had followed home. Bit of a weird lot, Cassie thought to herself. All types and ages, but none as young as her. And, surprise, surprise. Mrs Jones had a man living with her. Her "Star Boarder" one of the girls whispered to her. "Don't get on the wrong side of Mr Ed If you want to stay in Jonesy's good books," Cheryl had advised. "He might be Polish and as ugly as a hat-full, but she thinks the world of him. Reckons he keeps all us girls under control. What a joke."

They all quickly melted away to attend to their various pursuits, some to the lounge, one to the movies with her boyfriend, and a couple to work. Without being asked, Cassie set about helping to finish clearing the table.

"You can leave all the clean stuff on the table Cassie dear," Mrs Jones instructed. "A couple more might turn up yet, including Angie I hope. Oh, and Mr Ed too. I suppose someone's told you about him eh?" Noticing Cassie's embarrassment she added, "Yair, I thought so. Well, when I said all the boarders were females, I wasn't including him. He lives with me you see. He earns his keep in other ways," she said with a wink and a chuckle. Again she cast a glance at Cassie and noticed she was blushing. My God, hasn't she got a lot to learn, she thought to herself.

The sound of voices in the foyer saved further explanations, and then a couple burst into the room laughing at some shared joke. Hands on hips, Mrs Jones feigned indignation.

"Well you're a fine pair aren't you, coming in here when we're all packed up? Think this is an all night diner or something do you? And just when I was telling our new resident how punctual you all are too."

"Aw come on Freddy. Don't go crook on us," the man said, as he came around the table and gave her a friendly hug. "Some of us have to work for a living you know."

"Oh so now cooking and washing for all you mob isn't working eh?" she said. But by now she was smiling, and, giving him a push towards the stove added, "Go on then. Your tea's in the oven. Get yours too Angie and then you can meet my new helper. Not that I need one apparently, according to the hard working Mr Ed."

With their meals on the table, she introduced them to Cassie. Eddie Polanska was a rather rough looking middle aged man with the skin of a manual worker, Cassie noticed as she shook hands. She was to find out later that he was indeed a builder's labourer, and that he had adopted the name of Eddie because his polish name had nine letters in it and was too hard to pronounce. He and Mrs Jones were obviously very comfortable together. Two of a kind, Cassie thought.

Angie appeared to be a few years older than herself, and much more sophisticated. Her spikey hair-do and classy dress made Cassie feel a bit intimidated but she seemed to be friendly enough. Mrs Jones flopped into a chair at the table and motioned for Cassie to do the same.

"Angie here's a hairdresser, aren't you dear?" she asked.

"I will be in a year's time Jonesy, when I finish my apprenticeship," she replied. "I can't wait to earn some proper money."

Mrs Jones gave Cassie a wink. "Well how would you like to stretch your pay a bit further in the mean time? Cassie here is in drastic need of a bed and I wondered if you would mind sharing with her for a week or two till someone leaves. She's going to be giving me a hand to look after you mob. She'll pay half the rent, won't you dear?"

Angie glanced at the traumatised girl across the table and wondered what on earth she was doing working as a flunky in a place like this at her age. She seemed to be harmless enough, and the saving on her rent would come in handy. Jonesy would make sure she didn't step out of line. She gave a friendly smile.

"Sure," she said, "but I hope you haven't got too much gear Cassie. There's not a hell of a lot of space in that cubby-hole Jonesy advertises as a "large airy room."

"Get out with you, you cheeky bugger," Mrs Jones said, pretending to take a swipe at her, but breaking into her friendly cackle at the same time. "You were pleased enough to take it when you came here on your first year's wage eh? As for gear, all Cassie will be bringing is over there," she said, indicating the stuffed sports bag near the door. "I'll get Ed to put up a spare bed and set of drawers."

Then, bouncing up and heading for the sink, she said "Get a wriggle on you two so we can get cleaned up here. Come on Cassie. You can start work right now. We'll work out how much I'm going to pay you tomorrow. It'll have to be enough to cover half Angie's rent or she'll kick you out real fast. Real little terror for money is our Angie." She cackled away at her own humour as she plunged her hands into the suds.

CHAPTER FOUR

As the first rays of dawn filtered through the curtains at the window, Cassie lay awake listening to the city come alive. The hum of traffic started to increase in intensity. A garbage truck moved in staccato bursts along the street, pausing to heave the contents of each bin into its cavernous innards before sidling up to the next one of the dozen or so standing sentinel like on the footpath. Somewhere in the distance a clock chimed six times, and from a room down the hall an alarm clock shrilly tried to wake its owner.

"You awake?" Angie whispered from her bed.

Cassie rolled over to face her. "Sure am. Is it okay if I get up now? I should be getting down to help Mrs Jones with breakfast."

"Go for your life," Angie replied. "I get up now anyway. Cheryl's alarm wakes me every morning so I go to work early. Keeps me in good with the boss too, which doesn't hurt. It earned me a good bonus last year. You'd better get a wriggle on if you want to get first go at the bathroom."

By the time they had moved in furniture and settled Cassie in the previous night they were both ready for bed. Angie was very friendly and helpful and didn't seem at all put out by the request to share. She was a country girl from a big family and eager to have someone to talk to for a change. They chatted as they lay in bed with the light off.

"You might think it couldn't possibly be lonely in a place like this Cas," Angie had said, "but, believe you me, it can be. Most of the others are older than me, and we really only see each

31

other at meal times. If it hadn't been for Mrs Jones I would have died of loneliness when I first came to live here. She looked after me like a mother at the time. I think she will for you too. She seems to really regret not having kids of her own."

"I already think I've been very lucky to find her," Cassie said softly in the darkness. "And you. Thanks for having me."

There was a pause and then Angie asked "If you don't mind me asking Cassie, how old are you?"

After hesitating a few seconds she replied rather sheepishly "I'll be sixteen soon. Next month in fact. What about you?"

"Just eighteen, but I was only your age when I came here. One of my sisters stayed here years ago, so I knew it would be okay, but what about you? How did you find us?" She thought she heard a sob come from the camp-bed across the room. "Sorry," she said. "None of my business."

Maybe it was the security offered by the dark room, or perhaps she detected a kindred spirit in her new room-mate, but for whatever reason, Cassie felt compelled to confide in her. She let her whole story spill out, her childhood, her school, her mother, her desperate search for a job. The lot. Angie listened in silence until she had finished.

Perhaps reflecting on her own happy family situation, Angie felt incredible pity for the poor lost soul in the other bed. "Thanks for telling me that Cas," she said with such sincerity that it was not missed by Cassie. "Between Jonesy and me, we'll look after you. Things can only get better for you by the sound of things."

"I hope so," was the whispered response. They both lay in silence with their own thoughts until sleep overtook them.

After a quick trip to the bathroom Cassie hurried down to the kitchen, concerned that she might be running late for work on her first day. She found Mrs Jones busy frying bacon.

"Sorry I'm late Mrs Jones. You forgot to tell me what time I should start each morning."

"This is okay Cas. Cheryl's alarm seems to wake everyone at six so they all start coming in for breakfast from about half past. Mr Ed's already had his and gone to work. Boy, can that man eat, but there's still a bit left for the rest of you," she said, indicating a warming dish with bacon and eggs in it. "You'd better grab some before the others hit the place."

Cassie met the remaining residents as they had breakfast, and scurried about trying to be helpful to her boss. Most of them made sandwiches to take for lunch and selected something from a large bowl of fruit. How lucky they are Cassie thought, with memories of the last few days of hunger still fresh in her mind.

When the dishes were done and the kitchen was back in order they set about washing the bed linen from a third of the rooms which was left in the hall on a rotation system each week. The long clothes-line in the back yard was eventually draped with sheets and pillow-slips from one end to the other. By lunchtime Cassie was exhausted.

"Time for a cuppa don't you reckon?" Mrs Jones asked. "I'll put the kettle on. You make yourself a sandwich Cas. You must be hungry."

"I sure am," she replied. "However did you handle all this on your own?"

Mrs Jones gave a chuckle. "Oh I generally have someone around the place to help me. Even Mr Ed sometimes, but generally one of the girls staying here. Not all of them work full-time you know, but most of them think it's below their dignity to do a bit of house-work. Wait till they get married. They'll be in for a rude shock then."

"Well you don't have to worry about that in my case Mrs Jones," Cassie said. "I've always done most of the house-work at home, and I really appreciate the chance to have a job. Any job."

Mrs Jones frowned to herself as she set two mugs on the bench and fetched milk from the fridge. This girl had her worried. She was much younger than most of her residents and seemed to have come out of the blue. It was time to find out her story, she decided.

"Coffee or tea Cassie?"

Although she didn't normally drink either, Cassie decided it was time for her to grow up a bit if she was going to act as an adult.

"Coffee thanks Mrs Jones. Can I make you a sandwich too? Cheese and tomato okay?"

"That would be lovely thanks."

When they were settled at the table Mrs Jones observed her young companion as they ate. Noticing the shudder as she sipped her coffee, she pushed the sugar bowl towards her.

"Here. A bit of that will make it more drinkable."

She looks terribly uncomfortable, she decided. Perhaps she's in trouble with the law. Couldn't have that going on in this place. She decided to bite the bullet.

"Cassie, if you're going to stay here and work for me I need to know a bit more about you. Have you let your parents know where you are?"

A shake of the head.

"Don't you think you should? They'll be worried sick you know."

"No they won't," she stated flatly. "I haven't had much to do with my father for years, and my mother is more interested in her new man than me. She'll get over it." She paused to take another sip of her coffee. "I don't want to talk to her. She'll just send me back to boarding school. I hate it, and I'll just run away again."

Freda Jones eyed her new recruit over the rim of her cup. She recalled her own unhappy childhood and the final slanging match with her mother that led to her walking out too, never to return. It was weeks before she rang to let her know she was alive and would not be coming back, but over the years she regretted her action. It must have been hell for her mother. Her gaze returned to the nervous young girl in her charge who was concentrating on her sandwich.

"I think you should Cas," she said at last. "Just let her know you're okay. You needn't say where you are."

Another shake of the head and a very determined face. They sat in silence for a while. Then Mrs Jones reached across the table and took her hands in her own.

"Listen to me Cas. I know how you feel, but I'm right. If you want to stay here you're going to have to go along with me on this, but if you like, I'll do it for you." She watched panic fill her eyes. She held up her hand. "No names or addresses. Just a message to say you're safe, have a job, and somewhere to stay. I'll hang up if she tries to question me. How about it?"

This time a nod of the head.

"Okay? Good. Now give me the number and I'll duck down to the public phone box to make the call so it can't even be traced. Just in case eh? Here. Write it on this," she said plucking a serviette from a pack on the table. Cassie wrote her mother's name and number on it and handed it to Mrs Jones.

"You just wait here for me," she said, heaving her ample body from the chair. "I won't be long. Make yourself another sandwich. You look like you could do with it. If you're going to live with me you'll have to fatten up a bit my girl. You make me feel embarrassed," she added, patting her bulging hips and chuckling to herself as she left.

❧

Cassie waited nervously for her to return. She could just imagine the heart wrenching story her mother would tell Mrs Jones. How she and Aldo were distraught and would do anything to get Cassie to return home. Of course she wouldn't have to go back to that school if she didn't want to, Angela would say. Not much, Cassie muttered to herself. Anyway the thought of living with her mother and Aldo was no more appealing than the school. The front door opened and closed and footsteps came up the hall and into the kitchen.

"What did she say?" Cassie asked as she wiped the last cup and hung up the tea-towel.

"Like I promised, I didn't give her a chance to ask anything Cassie," Mrs Jones stated, looking her squarely in the face. "I just said 'Cassie's staying with me. She's safe and I'll look after her,' and then I hung up before she had a chance to quiz me."

Cassie breathed a sigh of relief and produced a wan smile.

"That would have nearly killed her with frustration. Thanks Mrs Jones. I just couldn't face talking to her. Not yet anyway."

"That's okay. At least it might stop her sooling the police onto you. Now, let's finish up here and then we'll have a spell for a while. I don't suppose you watch the soaps, but I do and you're welcome to join me if you like. You might learn something from Dr Phil. He handles lots of unhappy family situations you know," she added, only half jokingly.

Together they went to the lounge and spent a couple of hours watching afternoon shows. At least Cassie did, as her boss almost immediately fell asleep and, with mouth wide open, snored her way through most of the program. She gradually relaxed, confident she could trust this new person in her life. What a pity my mother isn't more like her she thought. We'd still be living happily as a family. I wonder if she'll tell Dad what's happened.

A particularly loud advertisement for cars jolted Mrs Jones awake. "Oh my God," she exclaimed. "I thought I was getting run over. Must have dozed off for a minute or two eh? Never mind. Probably wasn't worth watching anyway."

Then, glancing at the clock on the TV she scrambled to her feet. "Just look at that time Cas. We've got to get cracking. I've got to put a leg of lamb in the oven. How about you bring that washing in and fold it up for me eh? Then we'll have a nice cup of tea. Unless you'd prefer coffee," she said as she headed for the kitchen laughing.

Cassie smiled to herself as she made her way out to the clothes-line.

CHAPTER FIVE

That night Cassie saw her for the first time—the girl she had followed to her new home. She was one of the eight who turned up for dinner, but she showed no sign of recognition. Good, thought Cassie. She can't have noticed me following her and her boyfriend. She wondered what Mrs Jones thought of them bringing males into the place. Her name was Rebecca, or Becky for short, Cassie was pleased to note. That said something for her.

Later that night they found themselves alone in the lounge when the others had all disappeared. Cassie was jolted from her drowsy television viewing when Becky, without taking her eyes off the screen said, "We saw you following us you know."

"Oh my God," Cassie said. She was mortified. "I'm so sorry. I didn't mean to be rude. I don't know what came over me." Fully awake now, she turned to Becky to find her still staring at the television, apparently not wanting to pursue the matter any further. Perhaps she should try to explain her actions. "Please forgive me Becky," she pleaded. "I was at my wits end with worry, and you just seemed to catch my eye. I don't know why. Please give my apologies to your boyfriend."

"Boyfriend," Becky exploded with a laugh. "Not bloody likely. I've got better taste than that."

Cassie was confused. They looked like a couple to her. "Oh, I'm sorry. I just thought...." She trailed off into silence.

Becky turned to cast a long appraising look at her.

"How old are you Cassie?"

Once again she felt compelled to try to cover her age. "Almost sixteen."

"And you've just run away from school Cheryl tells me. Boarding school no less. Must have been pretty bad huh?"

"It was terrible. I hated it."

Becky continued her cool appraisal of her companion. Not only young, she thought to herself, but naive too, even for a fifteen year old. Probably from some uppity family wanting to be rid of her. She wondered if it was her role to educate her in the facts of the real world, the one into which she had now stumbled. Maybe not, but she was going to have to grow up pretty fast now if she was going to survive in the Valley as a young girl. She reached for the remote.

"You're not watching this are you?" she asked.

"Not really."

"Let's make a coffee then," Becky said. "There're a few things you need to know if you're going to live at the grandly named Harmony Apartments."

While they made their drinks they exchanged information about their lives. Cassie told her about the problems in her life, and how she came to find herself wandering aimlessly in the Valley. Becky, who turned out to be only seventeen herself, explained how she had also run away when she was Cassie's age from a step-father who was molesting her. Fleeing her home in Sydney, she hitched a ride to Brisbane with an over-night truckie, and was lucky enough to find a job in a cafe. She too had stumbled onto Harmony Apartments after struggling to find any other affordable accommodation, and had been there for months.

Cassie was amazed at the similarities in their lives. Not that she had ever been molested, she thought, but both had felt compelled to get away from conditions they judged to be intolerable.

Back in the lounge clutching their mugs, Becky's coffee and Cassie's chocolate, they sipped in silence for a couple of minutes before Becky put hers down.

"Cassie," she said carefully, "If you're going to live here you'll find this out sooner or later, so I might as well tell you now." A look of apprehension spread across the young face watching her. "You see, that bloke who was with me when you followed us here was no boy-friend. He was a client."

She watched as realisation dawned and a blush rose to Cassie's cheeks.

"You mean you're..." She couldn't bring herself to say it.

Becky smiled at her embarrassment. "Go on. Say it. A prostitute. That what you want to know?"

"I'm sorry," Cassie Mumbled. "It's none of my business."

"No, you're right," Becky said, "but if you keep living here it will become your business. You see, I'm not the only one who supplements their income with a bit of easy money on the side. You'll see more than me bringing home a man from time to time."

"But I thought you worked in a cafe?"

"I do, but the pay's terrible. I couldn't get by on it. We're not professional prostitutes really. Just amateurs with a taste for the finer things in life," she added with a laugh. "Come on Cassie. Lighten up. You look like you've just seen a ghost. This is the real world you live in now, not some la-de-da girl's school."

"But, but, Mrs Jones," Cassie stammered.

Again Becky laughed. "We don't have to worry about her.

Jonesy had her share of over-night lodgers too, before Mr Ed arrived on the scene."

"But isn't she scared of getting caught. It must be illegal. She could get closed down."

Once again Becky laughed. "No, we're pretty safe. We all toss her some of our takings and she shares it with a certain cop at the Valley C.I.B. just to make sure they never come poking around in our neck of the woods."

She could see that Cassie was still stunned by what she had just heard. And shocked too, she assumed, but she'd learn. I was like her once too, she thought.

"Anyway," she said, rising to her feet, "I'm off to bed. On my own tonight," she added, smiling at Cassie's discomfort. "Maybe not tomorrow night though. I have my eye on a pretty little dress in the shop next to the cafe. Turn the light out when you go," she added as she swept out the door.

Cassie sat in stunned silence, her mind in turmoil over what she had just heard.

CHAPTER SIX

Two weeks later one of the residents left to travel overseas and Cassie was able to move into her room. As she packed her meagre possessions after dinner, Angie put down the book she had been reading on her bed, and swung her legs over the side to watch her. "I'm going to miss sharing with you Cas," she said. "It's been great having someone to talk to."

Cassie jammed the last item in her bag and zipped it shut. "Well you won't have to go far to visit me will you? I'll only be two doors away."

"Yes. I know. You're going to be next to Becky aren't you? I hope she doesn't keep you awake all night." She watched for a reaction. Cassie paused for a second, but said nothing. Maybe she didn't know. "You do know what she gets up to don't you?"

Cassie hid her embarrassment by concentrating on folding her sheets. Avoiding Angie's inquiring look, she simply said, "Yes. She told me."

"And?"

"Well naturally, I was shocked, especially with what she told me about Mrs Jones."

Angie laughed. "Jonesy? How do you think she managed to pay for this place? Not working as a hairdresser like me, that's for sure."

A strained silence hung in the air as Cassie finished doing her bed. A thought had just occurred to her. She turned around.

"Having me share your room hasn't been a problem for you has it Angie?"

Angie roared laughing. "Good God no!" she gasped. "I've never been that desperate for a few dollars. Not that I haven't been jealous when I've seen what Becky can afford to buy in the shops. She's not the only one either you know. How do you think Carmel got the money to travel overseas? Not from being a checkout chick at Woolies, that's for sure."

When she saw how uncomfortable Cassie was she was sorry to have made fun of the matter. After all, she is only fifteen, or almost sixteen she thought with a smile. Hopping up from her bed she said, "Sorry. I shouldn't joke about it. Here. Let me help you take your gear to your new room. I bet you'll appreciate the extra space for a change. And a decent bed instead of that stretcher." Then, as an after-thought, "even if it is probably nearly worn out. Oops sorry. There I go again."

❦

The room was not the best one in the building, being next door to the bathroom, and the window over-looked the alley at the back of the building rather than the front street. Cassie eyed the bed suspiciously as she lay her bag on it and began to un-pack.

Angie arrived with clean linen. "Well, what do you think?"

The smile on Cassie's face said it all. "I'm stoked," she replied. "No prissey school-girls. No snoring back-packers. What more could a girl want?"

"Well a better view, for starters," Angie said as she drew back the curtains, opened the window, and took in the delights of the alley and blank wall of the factory across it. "Phew! The fresh air's nothing to write home about either." Then, noticing Cassie's strained look, added, "Oops. I guess that wasn't too smart of me either."

Cassie joined her at the window. "That's alright," she said

quietly. "At least I'm out of your hair, and I'm just so pleased to have somewhere safe to stay. You know I was within hours of being out on the street when I came here. I'm just so grateful to Mrs Jones, and you too Angie. You've both been so nice to me."

"Rubbish. I've really enjoyed our time sharing, but I know how you feel. I was the same when I first came here. The feeling of independence over-shadows everything else doesn't it?"

Cassie put the last of her clothes in a drawer and pushed the bag under the bed.

"Come on," Angie said, throwing the linen on the bed. "Let's get this made up and then I suggest we go out for a celebratory cup of coffee. Or milkshake if you like," she added with a smile. "My shout."

❧

"Just look at that Becky will you?" Angie spluttered. They were seated in a coffee shop on Brunswick Street enjoying two lattes which Cassie found much more to her liking than Mrs Jones' home brew, especially when accompanied by a slice of very nice cheese-cake. She nodded at the couple laughing and joking as they walked hand in hand along the footpath outside the window. "Doesn't she have any pride?"

Cassie had seen it all before and she knew exactly where they were heading. As she watched them disappear around the corner, she remembered the night she had followed Becky home.

Dropping her gaze back to her coffee she almost whispered "I have Becky to thank for having found Mrs Jones, and you of course," she added with a smile.

"How come? I thought you didn't know anyone when you landed on our doorstep."

"I didn't, including her." She noticed the confused look on Angie's face. "For some unknown reason I followed her home one night when I was looking for work and somewhere to live. She had a man with her then too. I have no idea why I did it, but if I hadn't I wouldn't be sitting here with you now, that's for sure. I wouldn't have found my way to that street if I hadn't been drawn there following them."

"So she told you herself then? What she's up to, I mean."

Cassie concentrated on cleaning up the last few crumbs from her plate. When she answered, she couldn't meet her friend's eyes. "Yes."

"And you condone it?"

"I didn't say that Angie, but I do understand why she does it to a degree. When you're desperate I suppose you will do anything to earn some extra money."

"Desperate? Is that what she told you? She's not desperate. Just greedy is what she is. With tips, she probably earns more than I do, and certainly more than you, I bet. I'd starve before I'd stoop that low."

Cassie still had vivid memories of the position in which she had found herself only a few weeks before. She knew what hunger and desperation felt like and wondered if Angie did.

"I suppose it's easy for you to say that," she said. "Maybe if you really were starving you'd think differently."

Angie looked shocked. "Cassie! Don't you dare to even think like that."

"Of course not, but you probably haven't ever been in that position to know how you would react have you?"

"No, and I sincerely hope I never will. Anyway, we should be getting home. I have a couple of letters to write. Let's go."

⚜

Dinner was finished, but the girls all lingered around the table chatting as Cassie cleared the dishes and tidied up. Then a beaming Mrs Jones came in from the kitchen bearing a large cake with sixteen candles blazing on it.

"Happy birthday Cas," she shouted, and the others all joined in.

Cassie was embarrassed beyond belief. "Mrs Jones. You shouldn't have gone to this trouble. How did you know?"

Touching the side of her nose with a forefinger and winking playfully she said, "we have our ways and means of finding out. I'll tell you later, but for now, for God's sake blow out these candles so we can all get into this cake. It smells delicious, if I do have to say so myself. Now girls, all together.....Happy birthday to you, happy birthday to you, happy birthday dear Cassie, happy birthday to you. Hip hip hooray."

Later, as Mrs Jones washed and Cassie dried, she asked again. "So how did you find out Mrs Jones?"

"Before we get onto that, now you're sixteen you'd better start calling me Jonesy like all the others eh? As for your birthday, I rang your mother again."

Cassie almost dropped the plate she was drying. "You didn't! You promised me you wouldn't."

"I did no such thing young lady. On purpose, I might add. That woman might have acted in ways that don't suit you, but she is your mother and I'm sure she still loves you. And cares about you too. I know she does, because she told me so, and I believe her."

She wiped her hands on her apron and went to comfort Cassie who had collapsed onto a chair and was sobbing quietly.

"I'm sorry. I didn't mean to upset you Cas, but I know I'm right about this." She handed her a few tissues. "Here blow your nose and listen to me." She waited until Cassie had composed herself and sat red eyed beside her.

"You don't have to worry. I didn't tell her where you are or what you're doing. I just let her know that you were safe, being looked after, had a place to stay and a job with me. Then I had to spend ten minutes convincing her I wasn't running a paedophile ring," she added, with one of her throaty laughs.

Cassie smiled wanly, wondering what her mother thought of the very down to earth Mrs Jones.

"That's better Cas." She paused. "There was one other thing. I promised her I'd try to convince you to ring or write to her. How about it?"

Cassie looked aghast, but then relented and, with downcast eyes she whispered, "I probably will. Just give me a day or two to think about it please. And thank you Mrs Jones. I know you're only trying to help me."

Mrs Jones gave her a hug and headed back to the sink. "Come on now. These bloody dishes won't wash themselves you know. Oh, and for God's sake call me Jonesy eh?"

⁂

"Aldo! Aldo! Look what came in the mail," Angela shouted, as she ran into the living room waiving an envelope. "It's from Cassie. I know from the writing."

He put down his paper and said "well calm down woman and open it for Pete's sake. Then you can read it to me and we'll both know what's happened to her. Come and sit here," he added, patting the sofa beside him."

With nervous fingers, she ripped it open.

"Dear Mum," it says.

"Well that's a start," Aldo said, and unwisely added, "at least it didn't start dear bitch."

Angela gave him a disapproving look, and then clutching the letter to her bosom, rose and walked out of the room. "I think I'd like to read this privately first Aldo. I'm going to the balcony." There, with the blue Pacific Ocean stretched out before her, she started again. She was soon glad of her decision.

Dear Mum,

I am writing to let you know that I am well, that I am not in danger, and that I am not coming home. The lady I am staying with who rang you before insisted that I should write so you can stop worrying about me. I am working for her and she is looking after me. Please don't try to find me to send me back to that horrible school. I will only run away again if you do.

Maybe someday, if you ever get rid of that silly Aldo, I might consider coming home, but so long as he is the most important thing in your life, I'm happier here.

Love,

Cassie.

PS Please let Dad know I'm okay. (If you're still talking to him these days.)

There was no return address. Tears ran down her face as she read it a second time, then a third. She sat for some time staring at the sea until she was disturbed by a call from Aldo.

"Are you alright out there?" he called out.

"Yes. I'm coming now," she replied. Then she tore the letter into tiny pieces and shoved them in her bra. No way was Aldo going to see that, she thought.

CHAPTER SEVEN

Cassie sat on her bed with all her worldly wealth laid out before her in little piles. Fifty seven dollars and sixty cents she muttered to herself with disgust. After living and working here for two months that was all she had to show for it. Of course she had to buy some cheap casual clothes and other necessities in that time, and the girls were always asking her out for coffee and things, but she had been trying hard to save up and get ahead., Sadly, this was as far as she had got.

There was a knock at the door. "You in there Cas?" It was Becky.

"Just a minute," she called out. She quickly stacked it back in the chocolate box Jonesy had given her for her birthday and slipped it under the clothes in her bottom drawer. Then she let in her neighbour. She had become quite friendly with Becky over the last few weeks, although she was still somewhat in awe of her and her exploits with men.

"Come in Bec. You look nice. On the way out?" She was always nicely dressed, but tonight she looked even better than normal in an attractive black and white pantsuit and heels accompanied by matching gold choker and ear-rings. She always wore make-up too, even around the house. It made Cassie feel positively dowdy in comparison.

Becky took the only chair in the room and Cassie sat on the bed. "Yes. I'm going to see that new movie on at the Rex. Do you want to come? I can wait till you change."

"I'm sorry Bec. I'd love to but I can't I'm afraid."

"Why? Have you got something else on?"

Cassie thought about making up some feeble excuse, but nothing came to mind. Besides, she would be faced with the same situation again tomorrow, or next day, or next week. She couldn't avoid the issue forever, and Becky had sort of become a friend. Perhaps it was time to come clean.

"No. Absolutely nothing, but the fact is Bec, I can't afford it," she said. "Besides, I don't have any suitable clothes, and if I can't save up some more money, I never will have any." There, she thought. Unpalatable as it was, the truth was out.

" God Cas," she gasped. "I'm sorry. I didn't mean to embarrass you. I should have realised things would be tough for you, what with running away from home and all. You've had to start from nothing I suppose, and I bet Jonesy doesn't pay you too well."

"Don't blame her Bec. She's been very good to me. Did you realise that when I followed you home and ended up here that night I had nowhere to stay and virtually no money left. She saved my life. I'm happy here and now I'm trying to save up to buy some better clothes, but it's just going to take time."

Becky thought back to her own move to the city and how tough it had been for her too in those early days, even though she had a proper job and brought some good clothes with her. Poor Cassie probably only had what she wore from school and the few things she'd brought since for wearing round the house. She made a quick decision. Jumping up, she took Cassie's hand and pulled her towards the door.

"Come with me," she ordered. "I've got an idea."

She led Cassie into her room next door, and flung open her

wardrobe door. Rummaging through the row of apparel there, she pulled out a burgundy pantsuit not too dissimilar to the one she was wearing, and held it up against her friend.

"There," she said triumphantly. "I thought so. You and I are the same height, but since I've put on a few kilos lately, this doesn't fit me any more, but I bet it would fit you like a glove. Like it? If you do, it's yours. What do you think?"

Cassie blushed as she pulled back. "It's lovely Bec. It really is, and it's kind of you to offer, but I can't afford something like that yet."

"Afford!" Becky chortled. "What do you mean afford? It's free silly. I told you, it's no use to me any more. I was going to give it to Lifeline anyway. Far better for you to have it than someone who wouldn't appreciate it."

"I don't know Bec. Besides, I've only got these school shoes. They wouldn't look too good with this would they?"

Becky could see the embarrassment this was causing Cassie. She looked for a way out.

"Tell you what Cas. Let me lend you some gear to fit you out tonight and we'll have a night out on the town. My shout. We'll talk about who owns what tomorrow. Come on. Say yes. It should be fun, and you deserve a bit of a break from this place."

Her enthusiasm was infectious. Twenty minutes later Cassie emerged in the pantsuit, heels, jewellery, and make-up that made her look years older. As Becky assured her, at least two or three years older.

"Wow! You look terrific Cas. Let's go and show you off to Jonesy, then we'll hit the town."

As it turned out, Jonesy wasn't all that impressed, although she was careful not to let on to the girls what she really thought. "I hope Becky doesn't influence that girl too much Ed," she said, when she returned to watching The Bill on television. "She's a bit too worldly wise for my liking. Cassie's still only a naive young schoolgirl really, though she doesn't look it tonight."

Ed was unimpressed. "I keep telling you Freda," he said, "what they get up to is none of your business. They aren't your kids you know, and they're all grown up women." After a pause he added "well maybe not Cassie, but she has to grow up one day too you know. Living around here, the sooner the better."

Jonesy stared sightlessly at the screen, recalling the poor frightened little girl who had knocked on her door only weeks ago and comparing her to the attractive young woman that Becky had turned her into tonight. She might not be her mother, but she had a mother's instincts towards her for some reason, and hated the idea of her going off the rails and getting into trouble. She shook the thought from her mind, took Ed's hand and pressed it to her lips.

"I know she has to dear, but I don't know if Becky is the best one of our girls to help her."

❧

"That was fun wasn't it," Becky said as they left the theatre and headed home. "Let's have a coffee at Mario's. My shout."

"It has been fun Bec, but I feel awful. First you lend me all these beautiful clothes, then buy the tickets to the movies. Please let me buy the coffees."

"You're on then Cas," she replied, "but stop worrying about that gear. I told you to keep it. It's no use to me any more. The shoes too. There's plenty more where they came from."

Cassie knew what she meant, but was too embarrassed to say anything. As they strolled along the street looking in windows, her thoughts returned to the night she had followed Becky and a man to what was now her home. At the time she was unaware of what they were up to, but she knew now and, thinking of where her nice clothes had come from left her feeling a bit self conscious. Still, she loved the feel of them, and hadn't failed to notice the admiring looks the two of them had been attracting all night.

As they chatted over their coffees she noticed a young man go to the counter. As he waited to be served he turned and scanned the room. Their eyes met, and he smiled at her. She quickly looked away and returned her attention to Becky who noticed her embarrassment.

"What's up," she asked.

"Don't turn around, but there's a man over at the counter looking at us."

But Becky wasn't like Cassie. She spun around, caught his eye and smiled back.

"Becky!" she whispered. "Do you know him?"

"No. Never seen him before, but I soon will." The look of abject horror on her friend's face made her laugh. "Chill out a bit Cas. He won't bite. Meeting him might be fun. There you are. I told you. Here he comes. Now be nice to him."

"Hello girls. Mind if I join you?"

"Of course not," Becky said, sliding into the alcove beside Cassie and leaving him her chair. "I'm Becky, and this is my friend Cassie."

"I'm Braith," he said, holding on to the back of the chair. "Can I get you girls another coffee before I sit down?"

They both answered at once, but Becky's "that would be lovely" won out over Cassie's "no thank you."

He laughed. "Well make up your minds girls. What is it? Yes or no? I don't want to be sipping latte on my own."

"Of course we will, won't we Cas? We're not in a hurry are we?"

Obviously uncomfortable, Cassie shook her head, and picking up her bag, slid out of the alcove.

"No, not for me thanks," she repeated. "I've got to start early in the morning," she lied. "I'll head home and leave you to it. Thanks for the offer Braith. Night Bec." She almost ran from the cafe.

⚬

Cassie stared into the darkness as she lay in her bed. What's wrong with me, she wondered. How embarrassing! Becky must think I'm a real prat. But she couldn't get the picture out of her head of Becky laughing and practically dragging that man home all those weeks ago. She wondered if she could ever be like her. Even those bitches at school used to tease her over her lack of a boyfriend.

Not that Becky's men were boyfriends, she mused. Clients she called them, with good reason. But look where it got her. All those beautiful clothes and here I am, wearing her free hand-me-downs. If only I was game, that could be me, she thought. Becky must have been like me once. I wish.... but no. I don't think I could.

Her thoughts were interrupted by whispering outside her door. "Shush!" It was Becky. "Don't wake everyone up. Specially Cassie. She's got an early start, remember." Then giggling, and the sound of a door opening and closing.

Cassie felt ashamed of herself, but she couldn't help it. She lay in the darkness straining to hear the noises from the next door room. Whispers, giggles, rustles, squeaks and finally moans. In her mind she followed the activity next door. She wasn't completely naive. Aldo and her mother made no effort to keep their love-making quiet. She had often listened in, excited, but also somewhat terrified even then. Now, here she was again, experiencing that same mixture of feelings. Eventually a door opened, then more whispering, and the sound of footsteps receding down the hall.

Sleep was slow to come, as she lay going over all that had happened on the most exciting time she had experienced since running away. All the emotions swelled up inside her. Embarrassment, shame, excitement, fear, and finally, just before she fell asleep, determination. Tomorrow was a new day, and she was absolutely determined to change her life. No more frightened little schoolgirl. From now on she was going to be more like Becky.

❦

It took a few more weeks, gradually becoming more out-going and adventurous. She even went on double dates with Becky a couple of times, and gradually her self confidence grew. And then it happened. She saw the most beautiful dress she had ever seen in a boutique window. It sparkled and danced before her eyes, and she couldn't get it out of her mind. Nor the price. It was well beyond her means.

"Just look at it Bec. Isn't it marvellous? I'd give anything to be able to buy it."

"Anything?"

"Pardon?"

"I asked if you would give anything to get it. If you meant what you said, well you know the answer don't you?" Becky fixed her with a steady gaze. "Cassie, you may not like it, but you know how I afford all the nice things I want in life don't you? It's up to you. Are you up for it? If so, I'll help you, but you've got to want it badly enough."

Cassie stared at the dress as thoughts and emotions clashed in her mind. Finally she turned to Becky, met her gaze, and said in the firmest voice she could muster, "Yes. I think I am. I want that dress."

CHAPTER EIGHT

As he shouldered his way through the door and spilled out onto the footpath, she actually ran head-long into him, causing him to fall, as she looked over her shoulder to see if the young man was following her. He wasn't. He stood watching her from the opposite side of the street.

"I'm terribly sorry," she said, taking him by the arm and helping him to his feet. "I should have watched where I was going. I'm really sorry. Are you hurt?"

"No. Not at all. Don't worry about it." He looked across the street in time to see the young man give one final glare in their direction before he stomped off down the street. She was watching too, he saw. "Was he bothering you?"

"No," she said uncertainly. Then, seeing the look of disbelief on his face, she blushed and looked at the ground. "Well actually, yes he was, but it was my fault. I'm sorry to have troubled you," she said as she turned to leave.

"Wait," he said, laying a hand on her shoulder. When she turned to face him, he saw tears running down her cheeks. She started to sob, and he pulled her to his shoulder where she cried silently. Eventually she stopped and tried to pull back, embarrassed at what she had done.

"I'm sorry sir. I don't know what came over me."

He held onto her arms and looked at her tear stained face.

"Please, stop saying you're sorry. There's no need to be. I can see you're upset. I'm just glad I could be of help. Are you okay now?"

She cast a nervous glance up and down the street. "Yes. I think so," she said.

He also checked out the street. The young man was nowhere to be seen. He relaxed his grip and smiled kindly at her.

"My name's Harry Elliott, and you can rest assured, I'm too old to be a danger to young women like you," he said to reassure her. "How about we pop inside and get you a drink of water or something eh? Tea or coffee if you like, just in case that fellow is still hanging around somewhere. I gather you don't want to see him again?"

She looked up and down the street again. "Would you mind? I'm so s.... Oops, there I go again." Then, offering her hand to him, she said, "That would be lovely Mr Elliott. I'm pleased to meet you. My name's Cassie."

He held the door open for her and they returned to his table where he pulled out a chair for her.

"Oh there you are Mr Elliott," Suzy said, coming over to them. "I wondered where you went. Do you wish to finish your dinner? I can get you some more if you like."

"No thanks Suzy, but you could bring us something to drink please? Tea as usual for me and, what would you like Cassie?"

"Just water thanks Mr Elliott."

He nodded to Suzy who headed for the kitchen. Turning back to Cassie he said, "I know I'm old enough to be your father, but I wish you'd call me Harry. I appreciate your good manners but Mr Elliott makes me feel ancient."

She smiled shyly at him. "Thanks Harry. I'm sorry."

"There you go again," he said. "Actually, I'm the one who should be saying sorry to you. I have to admit to the fact that I was spying on you across the street. I couldn't help seeing what happened. He was turning nasty, wasn't he?"

Cassie struggled with her answer. She owed this man an explanation, that was for sure, but she was ashamed of what she had done, and even more so for what she would have done if she hadn't changed her mind at the last moment. In spite of all her resolution, when it came to the crunch, she just wasn't game. Or maybe she just woke up to herself. No fancy dress was worth it. She had been a fool, and now she owed this kind man an explanation.

"It wasn't his fault," she whispered, unable to look him in the eye. "I changed my mind."

She took a gulp of the water that Suzy silently placed in front of her. Harry stirred some sugar into his tea.

"Look you don't have to explain anything to me if you don't want to Cassie," he said. "It's none of my business, but you seemed to be in trouble and I wanted to help if I could."

"I saw you watching," she admitted. "Through the curtains. At first I resented it. I thought it was none of your business."

"Which it wasn't," he interrupted.

"Maybe not, but you saved me from doing something silly that I would probably regret for the rest of my life. Thank you for caring"

"Well thank you is better than sorry, that's for sure." He wondered how to go on, or even if he should, but if he could do more to help this girl, he should, and she seemed to be accepting of his interest. It was worth a try.

"Cassie, as I said, I'm probably as old as your dad, but I've never been married so I don't have a daughter of my own, but if I did, and if she was in a spot of trouble, I would sure welcome any help she could find, even from some old busy-body like me," he gushed.

She stared steadily at him as she considered what to say. He seemed to be just a kindly old gentleman, and in some strange way, he did remind her of her dad. He would probably go out of his way to help a stranger in trouble too. Besides, she would never see him again, so what did it matter what he thought of her.

"I ran away from school," she said simply. He said nothing, but she thought she could detect sympathy in his eyes, so she continued. "And my mother."

It took her half an hour, but she told him the whole story of her life, and was surprised at how easily it all came out. He sat patiently sipping his tea and listening attentively. When she finished with her race across the street finishing virtually in his arms, she could hardly believe how cathartic the experience had been. She realised she had not told a single person the whole story, even Jonesy. It made her feel justified somehow in every thing she had done. Almost everything, she reminded herself. She should never have let envy and greed entice her to follow Becky onto the street.

Harry listened spell-bound. What a tale. This poor girl didn't deserve to be in the position in which she found herself. He found himself disliking her mother, feeling sorry for her father, and thankful to Mrs Jones for what she had done for her. So far, he thought. She had taken her in off the street and given her a job, but it was one with no future. This girl was better than that and deserved more from life than being a servant girl in a place of very doubtful repute. He wished he could help her. Well maybe he could, if he kept in touch.

"Cassie," he said at length, "I want you to promise me something." She looked at him expectantly.

"Will you promise to keep in touch with me? I'm a simple man, but I may just be able to help you in some way one day. I make a good shoulder to cry on if nothing else eh?" he said, trying to lighten the atmosphere.

He was pleased when she nodded and smiled at him. "I'm so s... embarrassed about that Mr...sorry, Harry," she said, and they both laughed. "Of course I will. If you give me your address I'll write to you, and you can rest assured, I've learnt my lesson tonight. I won't try that trick again."

"Good girl. Now, if you're ready to go home, I insist on walking with you, just in case that young man is still hanging around somewhere. You never know, and he looked like a nasty piece of work to me."

He wrote his address and phone number on a serviette. She put it in her bag.

"Come on," he said. "Let's go. I'm busting to see this Harmony Apartments place where you live."

Cassie laughed. "I wouldn't get too excited if I were you. As I said, it's a bit of a dump, but it's home for me at the moment. I wonder what my mother would think of it. Not really. I know exactly what she would think."

While he said nothing, Cassie's fall-out with her mother worried Harry. He understood to a degree how she felt. His own mother had taken him away from his father when he was only a baby, and though she did her best at raising him as the only child of a single mother, he always felt there had been something missing in his life and he suspected it was probably the lack of a father figure.

Maybe this would be the last he would see of Cassie, but he hoped not. As they trudged through the back streets of the Valley he dared to dream that in some way he could help her. How, he had no idea, but there and then he decided he was going to try.

CHAPTER NINE

A week later a letter arrived simply addressed to Cassie, c/- Harmony Apartments, The Valley. Her hands trembled as she took it from Mrs Jones. Someone had found where she lived. She would have to move on.

Back in her room she ripped open the envelope and breathed a sigh of relief when she saw who it was from. Of course. He knew where she lived because he had seen her home on that night that she was still trying to forget.

She had written to him next day to thank him and to apologise once again for her actions, but had purposely not included her address. She smiled as she remembered how amused he had been with the name when he saw the building that night. No wonder he remembered it. Relaxed now, she read the neatly written words.

Dear Cassie,

I hope you don't mind my writing to you, and you can rest assured I won't divulge your whereabouts to anyone without your permission, but there are several things I wanted to say to you. Please accept my suggestions as the clumsy attempt by an old man trying to be helpful. If you tell me to mind my own business I will fully understand and make no further attempt to contact you in the future.

Since you told me the story of your life the other night I have spent many hours thinking about what you said. What I want to tell you is that my life was badly affected by a similar family breakdown when I was only 2 years old, so I know from experience the impact it can have on your life. I blame it to a degree for the fact that I never found a wife or had children, and I deeply regret that shortfall in my life.

My mother was the opposite of yours and supported me all through my life until she died a few years ago, but unfortunately, I never knew my father. It left a hole in my life, and has eaten away at me ever since. It's silly, I suppose, but I still feel his loss today. You are fortunate to have two parents, both of whom I am sure love you in their different ways. For your sake, if not for theirs, please don't throw away the comfort and support that only a family can bring to each other. Your mother's boyfriend, Aldo I think you called him, may not always be there but your mother and father will be. This advice to you from an old man who knows is to find some way to reconnect with both of them, even if only by correspondence initially. I'm sure that as time goes by you will come to thank me for it.

Enough of my free, but un-requested, and probably unappreciated advice. I also have taken the liberty of putting some thought into your employment situation. You are too good to be a domestic for the rest of your life, although it has served a purpose for you in the short term. I have no idea what you aspire to do in the future, but, if you are interested, I am aware of a position becoming available for a receptionist. I think you would be perfect for the job, and the good news is, you would be working for a friend of mine. If you are at all interested, please write or ring so I can make arrangements for you to meet with him.

Thank you for your letter. I'm just glad I happened to be there for you when you needed a shoulder to cry on. It's now time to put that night behind you. We all make mistakes from time to time. Fortunately, you pulled out in time. You should be proud of yourself Cassie, not ashamed. I just wish I had a daughter like you.

Sincerely

Your new friend

Harry

P.S. You never told me your last name!

Cassie read the letter for a second time, tears welling to her eyes. What a kind man she thought. Again she was reminded of her father for some reason, although they were totally different in so many ways. Poor old Dad, she thought. It wasn't his fault he was totally obsessed with his farm. It was all he had ever known, or wanted to know. She wondered if he was even aware that she had run away. Of course he would be. It was the first place her mother would have looked for her. Then another thought struck her. Would her mother have told him she had contacted her through Mrs Jones and was safe and well? Probably not. She must write to him.

As for her mother, well that was another matter altogether. She had found the lifestyle she wanted too, but it didn't appeal to Cassie. Maybe she should try to be more sympathetic towards her. After all, life on the farm for someone like her must have been sheer purgatory for her once her dreams of becoming a member of the squattocracy failed to eventuate. Still, that didn't give her the right to destroy all their lives by splitting up the family.

Not that it would have worried her brother too much she decided. Cameron had headed for Thailand as soon as he finished school, and had hardly surfaced since. But then again, maybe that was why he chose that lifestyle. He wasn't like that when they lived on the farm, and maybe if they had stayed there he would be home on the tractor now instead of getting up to heaven knows what in South East Asia. Maybe the loss of his father had affected him like it had Harry Elliott. Then again, maybe not. He had always tended to be much more like their mother in nature. Selfish and self centred. He quite liked living on the Gold Coast. He even thought Aldo was great. Good luck to him, she decided. I hope he stays in Thailand. Dad wouldn't want him at home.

Home she thought. Yes, the farm was still home for her, and she thought that one day she would try to visit her father, but not yet. Maybe when she turned eighteen and became an adult in charge of her own life. In the mean time, she thought, I must write to him. She headed downstairs to ask Jonesy for a pen and paper.

⁂

Two nights later she met with Harry in Mario's. Up until his suggestion about the receptionist job she had given little thought to her longer term future, content for the time being to have free board, lodging, and a small wage, but she realised she would have to move on some day. Ambition was starting to take the place of survival at the forefront of her mind. Perhaps this could be the chance for her to take that first step. School was not an option. She wanted to earn some real money. At this stage she hadn't a clue how, but it would not be working the streets like Becky, she thought with a shudder.

Harry was waiting when she entered the shop. He rose as she approached and pulled out a chair for her.

"Hello Cassie. It's good to see you again," he said. "Bit better circumstances this time eh?" he added with a wink and a smile.

"Don't remind me Mr Elliott. I'm still ashamed." She lowered her eyes. "You must think so poorly of me. I'm surprised you are still trying to help me. I don't deserve it."

"Rubbish," he snorted. "Of course you do. You made the decision to run. I just happened to be in the way."

"I'm sorry."

"There you go again. I think sorry must be your other name."

He paused and looked at her seriously. "You realise you will have to give all your details if you apply for this job don't you?"

"It's Douglas. Cassandra Douglas. It's not that I don't trust you Mr Elliott, but I'm terrified that my mother will find me and send me back to school. I'm only sixteen you see."

"It's alright," he said reassuringly. "I'd guessed as much, but I think we can work out something to keep you safe from her, at least till you're eighteen anyway eh? If you get this job I'll talk to Craig about your situation if you like. He'll understand. He's a nice bloke, and a family man himself."

Harry watched her pondering her options. "Let me at least tell you about it," he said. "Would you like a coffee while we talk? I could do with one, and a slice of their great cheese-cake eh?" he said with a smile, not noticing the blood drain from her face as she recalled another night in this cafe when Becky's actions led her down the wrong path.

"Now let me explain where I'm coming from," he said as they waited for their refreshments. "I don't think I've told you, but I work at The General Hospital as a wardsman. I've been there for too many years to remember, and guess I'll be there till I retire now. It's not the greatest job in the world I suppose, but I'm single so I don't need much to live on. Besides, I like being able to help people when they're in trouble."

"Luckily for me," she interrupted.

He smiled. "Don't tell me you're sorry again will you? Anyway, probably because I've been there the longest I'm the union rep. on my floor, so I have to attend regular meetings with our Hospital's branch of the H.S.U. That stands for Hospital Services Union you know." She shook her head, so he continued. "I've become friendly with the Secretary, a fellow called Craig Thomas. He's a nice young bloke who'll probably make it to the top one day. He's very ambitious." He watched for her reaction.

"So what's the job?" she asked.

"It's receptionist. The current one is going overseas for six months. You would be handling the switch and front desk, doing filing and probably even acting as tea lady. Nothing very fancy I'm afraid, but you have to start somewhere. What do you think?"

Cassie turned the proposal over in her mind. The job sounded okay, better than the one she currently had for sure, but a couple of things worried her. Firstly, she was still worried about leaving the sanctuary of her anonymity at Harmony Apartments and the subsequent risk of being found by her mother. The second was the gratitude she had for Mrs Jones and how she had saved her from a life on the street. What would she think if I left her, she wondered, and if she did leave, where would she live.

"It sounds great," she ventured. "Where would I be working?"

"The Union has an office at the hospital. Do you know where the General is?"

"Yes. I've been there a couple of times. I just wondered if I could keep living with Mrs Jones if I took the job. I could pay her board like the other girls I suppose, but she would have to find a replacement worker for me and might need my room."

Harry weighed up carefully what he was about to say. He had given the idea a lot of thought but was still worried about how it might be taken.

"Cassie," he began tentatively, "I want you to consider something else while you're thinking about the job offer, something that on the surface might look just not right, but I assure you it is. Hear me out before you run away won't you?" he said with a nervous smile. "I'm going to suggest that you should come and live with me. No, that was badly put," he said, searching for the right term. "Not live with me in the usual context, but share my house, like flat mates."

He had been right to worry about her reaction, judging by the look of confusion and doubt on her face, but at least she hadn't slapped his face and run away.

"Let me explain." He went on. "As you know, I'm a bachelor and I live alone in a house at Windsor. It's no mansion, but it's comfortable, and only a short distance from the Hospital. I quite often even walk to work. I realise some people would think it improper for a young girl to be sharing with an older man, but I can guarantee you would be safe with me. I guess you would have to take my word that I have no ulterior motive in making this suggestion."

He paused, still pleased that she appeared to be listening to his case.

"Well actually there is a bit of an ulterior motive, to be honest. Living alone can be terribly lonely. It would be great to have someone to share conversation with away from work. From your point of view, I wouldn't be asking you to pay board or anything. Maybe help me with the housework though eh?" he added with a smile.

"Before you tell me what you think Cassie, there is one other point I want to make. While we have only known each other a few weeks, I have come to like and respect you for the nice young girl you are and I want to see you have a successful future. To be honest, I worry about the influences you come under at Harmony Apartments. Look how Becky could have led you to ruin your life, and while Mrs Jones had been kind to you, from what you've told me she does allow her home to be used for prostitution. One day she'll be raided, and all those living with her at the time will be caught up in it. I wouldn't like to see that happen to you. I think it's time for you to move on from there."

He looked earnestly at her as she sat staring into her cup as if waiting for an answer to appear there. Eventually she met his gaze.

"Harry, have I ever told you how much you remind me of my dad?" He shook his head. "That is just what I would have expected him to say. Not bullying me like my mother, but just offering good advice and hoping I was smart enough to see the value in it. Listening to you, I realised how much I miss him." Harry said nothing, waiting for her to go on.

"I wrote to him yesterday, after I read your letter."

"I'm glad," was all he said.

"I know you're right Harry. I've grown up a lot since I ran away from school, and I'm thankful for what my time in that place has taught me, but I want something better in life. I guess now is as good a time as any to move on. Nothing ventured, nothing gained eh?" she said with a wry grin. "If you think I could do the job, I'm ready to give it a go."

"And my offer?"

"It's very generous of you Harry, and I trust you. Of course I do, but would you mind if I did one thing before I give you my answer?"

He would never have guessed what it was, but he could not have been more pleased.

"I want to ring my dad, bring him up to date, and ask his advice. That's what I should have done long ago. You see, I now feel I can trust him too." She smiled brightly at him and added, "So. When can I see this Mr Thomas?"

CHAPTER TEN

Harry knocked and then pushed the door open as he stuck his head into the office. "Hello Craig. Can we come in?"

"Of course Harry. Take a seat. Oh, I see you need two," he said smiling at Cassie. "Who have we here?"

"This is Cassie Douglas, Craig, the girl I told you about. From the empty office out front I assume Helen had already left. Are you still looking for a replacement?"

Craig Thomas came around his desk and shook Cassie's hand. He was a good looking guy in his mid twenties, and she blushed at the warm pressure of his hand and the radiance of his welcoming smile.

"You can say that again," he replied. "Helen left last Friday and the place is a shambles already. Pleased to meet you Cassie. Please take a seat. Are you staying Harry?"

"No. I'll leave you to it Craig. I'm on duty back in Ward Three." As he left he noticed the apprehensive look on Cassie's face. He gave her shoulder a squeeze as he passed. "You'll be right Cassie. This bloke's a big softy really, and," he leaned towards her and said in a whisper loud enough for them both to hear, "he's desperate." Then, with a wink to Craig he left.

Years later Cassie would recall how well the interview went. Craig couldn't be nicer, doing his best to make her relax. He joked about his first job interview with one of the heavies in the head office of the union. Questions about her background and family situation were kept to a minimum, and he didn't seem too worried about her academic achievements, or lack of them. The interview went so smoothly that she later thought he must have made the decision to hire her when she walked through the door, and all the rest was just going through the motions. After less than five minutes he rose and ushered her towards the door.

"Come out to the front office and I'll show you what you'll have to do."

"Does that mean I have the job?" she asked, somewhat in amazement.

"Of course you do," he said. "Congratulations, but with Harry's recommendation, it was always a foregone conclusion, provided you want it of course. We haven't even discussed wages yet."

"Thank you Mr Thomas. I won't need much pay."
He laughed. "Hey, that's no way for an employee of a union to talk. You've got to learn to screw as much as you can from your boss you know. When can you start?"

⁂

Cassie didn't enjoy the thought of telling Jonesy she would be leaving, but bit the bullet while they were cleaning up that night. "I'm sorry to leave you in the lurch Jonesy, but he wants me to start straight away and I don't want to miss out on the job. How will you manage here?"

"Don't you worry about it Cas," she said with a chortle. "I managed before you came so I can do it again on my own if I have to, but something will turn up. It always does. You did, didn't you? This was just a chance for you to get on your feet, but you've got to get a proper job if you can."

Cassie threw her arms around her and gave her a kiss on the cheek. "Thanks Jonesy, for everything," she said. "You saved my life and I can't thank you enough."

"Oh don't be silly. You know I love helping you girls find your feet and move on in the world."

"There's something else Jonesy. Mr Elliott, you know, the man who organised the interview for me has suggested I could go to live with him in his house at Windsor. As a boarder of course," she added quickly when she saw the look Jonesy gave her.

There was a nervous pause in the conversation before the older woman spoke cautiously. "Cassie, you never did tell me how you met him. Do you know him well enough to trust him that much?"

The pause stretched even further as Cassie considered her answer. Then, hanging up her tea-towel, she said, "dry your hands Jonesy and come and sit down for a minute. There's something I have to tell you before I leave." Then, with a quivering voice, she told her of the night that Harry Elliott had saved her when she almost ruined her life. She also explained how he had convinced her to write to her dad, and she intended to ring him before she gave Harry her decision.

"So you see why I do think I trust him. He's just a lovely, lonely old man, trying to help me in his own way like you did when I came here. He's offered to let me stay there for free in return for helping him run the house, so I guess I'll still be doing the dishes and washing sheets," she laughed. "But that means I'll be able to save most of my wages. I'll be rich in no time," she joked.

Jonesy gave her a pat on the head as she struggled to her feet. "Unless you waste it all on buying fancy dresses eh?" she said with one of her trademark throaty laughs. "Now come on. Those dishes won't do themselves you know. When we're finished you can use the phone to ring your dad. I'm sure he'll trust your judgement too."

❦

"Hello Dad."

"Cassie! Is that you?"

"Yes Dad. It's me."

"Oh God! You don't know how glad I am to hear your voice. Are you okay? You're not in trouble are you?"

"No Dad. I'm fine. What about you?"

"You know me Cas. Same old, same old. Still missing you and Cameron after all these years."

"But not Mum?"

"Not so much. I've always worried what would happen to you kids after you all left here. I reckoned it might affect you in the long run. Why did you run away from school Cas? Bullying, was it?"

"Only partly. I don't suppose you've ever met Aldo have you?"

"Is he the latest toy-boy? No, not likely."

"How long is it since you've seen Mum?"

"Must be years. Why?"

"She's changed Dad. Living on the Coast with Aldo has turned her into a different person to the one we knew on the farm. I couldn't stay with them any longer. Do you understand?"

"Yes. Yes, I think I do Cas, but I wish you had come to me instead of disappearing."

"I'm sorry Dad. I really am, but if I had come to you I would have been sent back to her as she has custody of us. Then back to that crappy school. No thanks!"

"So where are you? Are you alright really? What are you living on?"

"Steady on. One question at a time. Actually, I'm writing you a long letter to explain all that's happened, but everything has turned out alright. In part, that's why I'm ringing."

"Go on then."

"I've been offered a job in an office, starting straight away."

"Well that sounds good. Are you going to accept it?"

"I think I will, but there's something else. I've made friends with a really lovely man."

"Oh God no Cas. You're only a girl."

"I'm sixteen Dad, but it's not like you think. He's your age. As a matter of fact, he reminds me of you in some ways."

"Poor old bugger. Go on then. It sounds like he'd be harmless."

Cassie had a mental picture of the crooked smile that would have broken across his face. "Don't be like that Dad. You know what I mean. Anyway, he arranged to get me the job interview. He works in the same place."

"Well that sounds all good. What's the problem?"

"No problem really, but he asked if I would like to share his house with him. He lives alone you see. He's never been married, and, besides being a great opportunity for me, it would help him too."

"How?"

"Company. I thought you might understand how he feels."

"Gees Cas. It sounds a bit risky to me. Are you sure you can trust him? He could be a real whacko."

"Dad, I know how it sounds, but I do trust him, and I'd like to accept his offer."

"Well that's up to you love. There's not much I can do about it is there?"

"There is actually. If I give you his phone number, will you do two things for me?"

"I'll try. What are they?"

"I'd like you to ring him and have a talk. I think you two would get on very well, but if you say no, then I won't do it."

"Fair enough. What's the other thing?"

"You must promise not to give his number to Mum. I don't want her annoying him and trying to track me down."

"But you trust me?"

"Yes Dad. I do."

"And I trust you too Cas. Of course I'll ring him if you want me to, but as I said, you're a big girl now. You have to make your own decisions from no on. I know you'll do the right thing."

"Thanks Dad. Here's his number. Have you got a pen?"

"Hold on a sec love."

Cassie heaved a sigh of relief as she waited. She knew her Dad would stand by her in spite of all the concern she had caused him.

"Okay. Fire away," he said.

She gave him the number. "And his name's Harry. I'll ring you tomorrow night to see what you think."

"Okay love. It's been great to hear your voice and to know you are alright. Please keep in touch."

"I will. Goodnight Dad. I love you."

Bill Douglas carefully placed the receiver in its cradle and stared at the number in front of him. His baby girl had grown up, and he hadn't been there to help her. She had to do it all on her own, but it sounded as if she was handling herself pretty well.

He wished he could do more, even at this late stage, but he had to honour his promise to let her make her own decisions. And not tell her mother, he reminded himself. Not that that would be hard. Since the divorce went through he couldn't remember a single contact.

Well now the kids had grown up and become independent, there was no reason to keep in touch. All that was in the past. Now here he was, on his own, even estranged from his kids. Not that he ever hit it off too well with Cameron. Too much like his mother, he was, but Cassie was another matter altogether. He felt a real rapport with her. Whatever else, he would do whatever he could to make it up to her. He could start with calling this man called Harry. He picked up the phone.

⅋

"Hello."

"Is that Harry?"

"Yes it is. Who's this?"

"Bill Douglas. Cassie's father."

"Oh Bill. It's good to meet you, so to speak. Cassie told me she was going to ring you. Did she give you my number?"

"Yes. Do you mind?"

"Of course not. I appreciate the opportunity to let you know what a wonderful daughter you have and how well she has handled herself. You should be very proud of her."

"Oh I am, but I'm also ashamed at what I must have done to contribute to her present situation."

"Rest assured, she doesn't blame you Bill. She thinks the world of you as a matter of fact. When she told me about you I suggested she should contact you. I hope you don't mind."

"Mind? Of course not. Is she really okay Harry?"

"Good as gold. You don't have to worry about that girl Bill. I suppose she told you I was able to organise a job interview for her?"

"No. She just said she had a job offer. Apparently she's going to accept it."

"Good. I hoped she would. She'll be working for a friend of mine in The H.S.U. office. He'll look after her."

"Talking about looking after her Harry, she tells me you have asked her to live with you."

"It sounds awful when you say it like that, but yes, I did suggest that to her. She said she wanted to talk to you first. Hence the call I presume. I suppose I'm being selfish really. I don't know about you, but I've found living on my own sucks at times. I'd love to have someone to share the house with me, but never seemed to find the right person. I think we could get on together, and Bill, there is no way you need worry about me making a move on her. I'm too old for that."

"Yair. Me too. I know what you mean. Look Harry, I don't quite know how to thank you for helping her like you have. If there's anything I can do for either of you, just let me know eh?"

"There is one thing. Write and invite us to come home for a visit. I'll drive her out there one weekend. I'd just love to see you two back together."

"She was right when she told me you were a nice man Harry. Get my number from her and keep in touch."

"Will do Bill. I've enjoyed talking to you too. Bye."

"Yair, see you mate. By the way, don't let her get too involved in that Union stuff will you? Her grandad would have a heart attack. Bye."

It was Sunday and Harry had picked her up in his car. After sharing a cup of tea with Mrs Jones she was loading her back-pack and two cardboard boxes containing all of her worldly goods into the boot. Besides insisting he should help her move, Harry had also wanted to meet the lady who had taken her in and looked after her when she needed her most. It was important to him that she trusted his motives in sharing his house with Cassie. He smiled to himself as he shut the door. They had got on okay, though she and her establishment were not his cup of tea. The sooner he had Cassie safely settled in with him the better, he thought.

Living alone gave him lots of time to think, and over recent days he had often found himself wondering at this latest turn in his life. Here he was fussing around concerning himself with the well-being of a young girl he had only met by chance a few weeks ago. He couldn't explain it, even to himself, but he had developed a real sense of responsibility towards her for some reason. Maybe it was because he had never married. Maybe she was the daughter he never had. He found himself really looking forward to her coming, and now here she was.

"Mr Elliott," she exclaimed as they pulled up in the driveway. "It's beautiful, and such a pretty garden. Do you look after it yourself?"

"Sure do. It's about my only hobby, growing things," he replied.

Cassie laughed. "It's no wonder you and Dad got on so well when you spoke to him then. It's his only hobby too, though on a different scale."

She put on her back-pack and carried the smaller box while

Harry carried the other and hurried ahead to open the door. He led her down the passageway and into her bedroom. A smug smile spread across his face as he heard her gasp as she entered.

"Oh my God!" she squealed.

"Like it?"

"Like it? I love it. It's beautiful. You've gone to so much trouble. You shouldn't have," she gushed.

"It was my pleasure," he said. "You deserve it, and I had to do something with the room. It's sat there empty ever since I moved in twenty years ago."

She put her box on the floor and gazed at her surroundings. The walls had been freshly painted a soft pastel pink, the ceiling a darker shade, and the floor sported a new grey carpet. Filmy white curtains framed the window. A polished timber wardrobe stood on one wall, and matching dressing table and mirror on another. The bed was covered with a pretty pink and grey check counterpane.

"It was my mother's," he said, as Cassie ran her hand over the glossy surface of the dressing table. "The house was too. I was her only child. She left it all to me."

She noticed the loneliness in his voice. It must be terrible to be all alone in the world, especially at his age. It made her think once more of her father. Both these men were keen to do what they could to help her. She wouldn't let them down, she decided, as she put her back-pack on the bed and turned to face him as he stood smiling in the doorway.

"I just don't know how to thank you Mr Elliott. I'll never be able to repay your kindness, but I'll try. What can I do to help you?"

"Well for a start, you can start calling me Harry instead of

Mr Elliott. Otherwise I'll have to call you Miss Douglas won't I? Now come and have some lunch. I hope you like it, but, being a bachelor, I've taught myself to cook pretty well over the years, if I do say so myself."

"Just as well," Cassie said, as she followed him into the kitchen. "I'm a hopeless cook, but I'm an experienced washer-upper."

"Sounds good to me," he said, standing aside and waving expressively at the sink which was covered in saucepans, pots and all the gear he had used in preparing a chicken casserole. "Be my guest."

CHAPTER ELEVEN

Later in life Cassie would reflect on what happened in her life over the next two years and wonder how much of it was her fault, how much was due to circumstances, and how much could be laid at the feet of others. Here she was, a naive young girl who should still be in school for two more years. Now she was thrust into the real world and forced to become mature beyond her years very quickly. Still, this was the path she had chosen for herself, and she was determined to make the most of the opportunity that Harry had organised for her.

She started work next day, arriving an hour before starting time because Harry gave her a ride and his shift started at seven. She used the time to familiarise herself with the layout of the hospital and its surrounds. It was a massive institution and the Union's office consisted of two rooms tucked away behind the administration centre. Two rooms and two employees, she discovered. Just herself and Mr Thomas.

He met her waiting outside and led her through the door and into the reception area.

"This is your station Cassie. It's a shame that Helen left last week. It would have been handy to have her explain the workings of the place, but I'm here on my own from time to time, so I'll do that as soon as I've made a call or two. How about you trot off to the canteen and get us some coffees? You'll find some petty cash in your desk." With that he headed for his office.

She stood, somewhat mesmerised by the situation, but

snapped out of it to call after him, "How do you like your coffee Mr Thomas?"

"Black, two sugar thanks."

Yuk! She thought as she rummaged through the drawer in the desk in search of the cash tin.

When she returned Craig joined her in the front office. He explained the operation of the phone and filing systems, and showed her how to access the computer programs. He could see she was getting flustered.

"You haven't done any of this before have you Cassie?"

"No."

"Can you type?"

"No."

"Would you like to learn?"

"Of course Mr Thomas. I'll pick it up. I know I will."

He stood considering her for a moment and then said, "I think we can do better than that. If you're willing, the union will pay for you to do a secretarial course. You'll end up with a diploma of some sort. Means more money for you too. Interested?"

She hesitated, uncertain. "Yes please," she said somewhat tentatively, "but are you sure it's okay for the union to meet the cost?"

He laughed. "Don't worry your head about that Cassie. I'm pretty much in charge of our expenses at this branch. Within reason of course," he added with a smile. "Just leave it to me. Now, let's get down to some work eh? You get familiar with the place till I call you. I have some calls to make." Then, as he headed back to his office, he paused and added, "Oh, and by the way, with only the two of us here, how about you call me Craig?"

The captivating smile he gave her was so friendly and welcoming Cassie felt a thrill run through her body. It was more than just relief that she felt comfortable with the idea of working with him. There was something else, but the thought never entered her head that her attraction was anything more than that. As she would find out over time, Craig had a dynamic personality. He exuded self confidence, almost bordering on arrogance, but that would only become obvious to Cassie when she had developed her own confidence as she matured. Today she was as nervous as a kitten, and just relieved that it seemed he would be easy to work for.

❦

Harry had been tossing an idea over in his head for days. Now it was time to decide. The weeks that had passed since Cassie came to live with him had been the happiest of his life, as far as he could recall. It never ceased to amaze him that an old man and a young unrelated girl could strike up such a friendship as the one they enjoyed. They found they actually enjoyed each other's company, and had even started socialising together, going to movies and on weekend drives. Suddenly, his life had meaning and value, but one disturbing thought would not leave his mind. He felt that he had stolen her from her parents.

Cassie had fully confided in him about her life and the family situation that resulted in her leaving school and choosing to head out on her own. He could understand, and even sympathise with her reasons, but, though he had never been a parent himself, he couldn't help feeling sorry for hers. It probably wasn't their fault. He understood family break-up was common these days, and that it quite often led to acrimony between the adults and the children involved.

Selfishly, he should have simply enjoyed Cassie's company

and not given her parents a second thought, but since he had spoken to her father, he couldn't get him out of his mind. He knew what it was like to live a lonely life, but how much worse it must be for a man who had had everything, and then lost it all. Bill Douglas seemed to be a really decent man. He didn't seem to deserve that to happen to him.

Under his urging, Cassie had taken to writing to her father weekly, and he noticed how keenly she looked for his replies, but, as far as he knew, she had made no effort to contact her mother. Well you had to start somewhere, he thought to himself. To be true to himself, he decided he was going to try to get her back with her family, starting with her dad, and therein lay his concern. From a purely selfish point of view, he dreaded the thought of losing her, even to him.

As they settled down to watch her favourite program, he put his idea to her.

"Cassie, it's only two weeks till Christmas. Is Craig giving you some time off?" he asked.

"Yes, he told me this morning. The office will be closed for ten days. Why?"

"I've been thinking. Would you like to spend that time with your father?" He waited expectantly while watching for her reaction.

She was thoughtful for a moment, and then said, "What made you think of that? Don't you want me here?"

"Don't be silly," he said. "Of course I do, but I've been thinking about him too. He must still be missing having his family around him at this time of the year."

"He has Grandma and Grandad."

"That must be fun," he said, and instantly wished he hadn't. "I'm sorry. I didn't mean that. By the way, how long is it since you've seen them?"

He thought she was ignoring his question, as she stared mindlessly at the screen for maybe a minute. Then she turned to him and he could see tears welling into her eyes. "Years," she replied. "Probably two or three. Cam and I went and stayed for two weeks so Mum and Angelo could go to visit his family in Italy." She paused again, and Harry let her take her time. Eventually she continued.

"I miss them. They were always lovely to Cam and me. I should write to them too, shouldn't I?"

"Better than that, why not go and visit them, like I said? You deserve to have your family back Cassie. It's all up to you. I'm sure they'd welcome you with open arms."

They both sat staring at the screen, but Harry could tell she wasn't really paying attention. The silence continued till the add break, then she hit the mute button and turned to him. The tears in her eyes had been replaced with excitement. They sparkled.

"On one condition Harry. You must stay with us too. I couldn't leave you here on your own. Not after all you've done for me. How about it? Is it a deal?"

In spite of all the objections he could raise, nothing was going to put her off. Of course her father would invite him, and her grand parents. Of course he would be able to get time off from his job. Hadn't he told her the other day that he hadn't had a holiday for years? No, her father didn't mind them sharing a house. He understood the situation and was dying to meet Harry actually. Of course his old car would make the distance. They only lived at Roma, not Rome!

Her excitement was contagious, and they found themselves laughing and chatting about the prospects until they realised their show was over and the next program started.

"That's it then," she said, jumping to her feet. "I've got a couple of letters to write."

She left Harry smiling contentedly to himself, content to leave the remote on mute as he contemplated how far she had come since that night he had watched her on the street. Me too, he decided. His boring lonely life had been transformed.

Then his thoughts returned to the uncertainty he had felt earlier in making the suggestion. It was selfish, he knew, but he hoped a meeting with her family would not bring an end to their new shared existence. Time will tell I suppose, he thought, as he flicked off the telly and headed off to make himself a cup of tea, and a cup of hot chocolate for Cassie. Seemed odd in December, but it was her favourite, and he loved to give her what she liked. He hummed quietly to himself as he warmed the milk.

2✦

Bill had done his best to prepare the cottage for his visitors. A cleaning service from in town had spent two days giving the place a good going over, while he spent his time making the garden as presentable as he could. It reminded him how lovely it had been in past times when he and Angela had shared the task of making it a show-piece. When she left, he couldn't see the point in trying to maintain it on his own and he had let it fall into disrepair. He had gazed in despair at his long ago abandoned vegetable garden that had once provided most of their needs. Again, it hadn't seemed worth-while growing things just for him and his parents. Still, he missed it. All his life he had just loved growing things, everything from barley to broccoli. Pity, but time moves on he decided, and turned his back on it to head for the main house for one more job that he had been putting off for days.

Now both in their eighties, his parents had been over the moon when he told them that Cassie would be spending Christmas back on the farm. They had never quite forgiven him for any part he might have played in the break-up of his family. True, they had always had reservations about the somewhat uppity young teacher he had taken for a wife. They had always assumed he would marry one of the nice farm girls from the local district, but in the end had decided any wife was better than none, which had started to seem to be the most likely outcome for him.

In time they had grown to be quite fond of Angela and had been devastated when she had packed up and left without so much as a goodbye, taking their precious grand-children with her. How they missed those kids. Since they left, life had lost its meaning, and they had drifted into old age with little interest in the farm or life in general.

Then there was the terrible business of Cassie running away from school. The worry of it had nearly driven them mad before Bill eventually told them she had contacted him and told him she was safe. But how could she be safe they had wondered, living alone in the city, and how could a girl like her support herself. It played on their minds for weeks, but gradually Bill had convinced them that she was able to look after herself.

But now they had something to look forward to. Their son had told them Cassie was coming to see them again. Dear little Cassie. How sorry they felt for her in particular. More so than for Cameron who was always much more like his mother. They wondered what they could do to make her visit memorable for her so she would come back again. Grandma Douglas settled on making one of her old fashioned Christmas puddings, even finding some old silver coins to put in, just like the old days. Grandpa retrieved some of his old vinyl records from the storeroom and cleaned up their old gramophone. A sing-a-long had always been a feature of Christmas Day. He found himself humming along with Bing Crosby to "I'm dreaming of a white Christmas."

"Yoo hoo. Anyone home?"

"Come in Bill," he said, turning off his machine. "Like a beer?"

"Thanks Dad. Mum in the kitchen? There's something I want to talk to you both about."

They settled in the lounge and chatted for a while. It hurt him deeply to see how excited they were about Cassie's visit, and to realise how much they missed her. He just hoped what he was about to tell them didn't spoil everything. His mother gave him the opening he had been waiting for.

"So when does she arrive dear?"

"Tomorrow Mum. They should get here late in the afternoon."

"They?" his father asked.

"Yes. That's what I wanted to talk to you about. Her friend is driving her and he's going to be staying too." He saw the worried look appear on his mother's face as realisation dawned on what he had just said.

"He? Surely she hasn't got a boyfriend, especially one old enough to drive a car. She's only sixteen Bill."

"No Mum. It's nothing like that. Harry's my age."

Her jaw dropped. "What! That's worse. Surely not our little Cassie?"

Bill chuckled at her suggestion that Cassie would be having an affair with someone in their sixties. "No Mum. Let me explain. Harry rang me weeks ago to ask if it was okay for Cassie to share his house with him." Again he saw the panic on their faces.

"He's the one who helped her to get the job I told you about, and he's been wonderful to her."

It was obvious that they weren't convinced, and he could understand why. He had taken a while to get used to the idea too, but in her letters to him over recent weeks Cassie had explained what she had done since running away from school, and how Harry's offer had enabled her to get out of The Valley. She spared him the detail on how she had come to meet her benefactor, but he had come to the conclusion that he could trust the man. Now he was going to meet him so he could judge for himself.

He forced himself not to smile at the looks of disapproval on his parent's faces. "Look you two," he said. "I know it may sound a bit suspicious, but I trust Cassie's judgement on this, and I think you should too, at least until we meet him tomorrow. I'm quite looking forward to it actually. He sounds very interesting."

They said nothing so he added, "Besides, how good will it be to have Cassie here for Christmas eh? Now cheer up. It will be alright."

He rose from his chair and picked up his hat. "I'm off to town to get some supplies. Is there anything you want me to pick up?"

His mother snapped out of the semi-trance she had been in. "Don't you go anywhere my boy until I make up a list. Anything to pick up? Only a heap of stuff, that's all. You can't prepare

Christmas lunch for five, including strangers, without some serious shopping. As a matter of a fact, I think I'll come with you. You'd probably buy more of that cheap No Name stuff you feed yourself on. Cassie wouldn't like that, nor her friend I'll wager, Mr....What did you say his name is?"

"Elliott. Harry Elliott. Sounds better than Aldo Mercini for a name don't you think?"

His mother hardly heard his answer as she was already scratching in the refrigerator, while his father had gone to check on the contents of his drinks cupboard.

Bill smiled smugly to himself as he settled back in the chair. That went off okay, he decided. Time will tell if they're still on side in a few days time.

❧

Harry's old Holden pulled up in a cloud of dust, as two kelpies rushed around barking and Bill hurried down the steps.

"Go and lie down," he shouted, and they retreated to their station beneath the tank-stand. Cassie poured out of the car and met him at the garden gate, throwing her arms around him and staying clutched in his embrace for some time.

"Welcome back Cassie," he whispered in her ear. "God I've missed you." He waited till her sobbing subsided, then held her at arm's length, while she frantically wiped tears from her cheeks and eyes. "Just look at you," he said. "You're not my little Cassie any more. You're all grown up."

She gave a strained laugh. "Well it has been two years Dad, and a lot has happened in that time."

"You can say that again," he said. "I'm just so sorry I wasn't there for you when you needed me, but I am now, believe me."

He suddenly remembered they weren't alone and looked at the man standing quietly beside his car. Pulling away from Cassie he headed towards him, reaching out to shake hands.

"I'm sorry Harry. She quite took my breath away for a minute. Pleased to meet you."

"And you too Bill," he replied, "although Cassie has talked so much on the trip out here I feel I know you pretty well already."

"That sounds like my Cassie," he said, as they followed her into the house.

※

The stay was a resounding success. They all loved Harry. He encouraged Bill to re-establish his vegetable garden, working for hours to build up the beds and get some seedlings underway, and he showed great interest in the operation of the farm, even though it was completely foreign to him.

They spent so much time together that Cassie found herself almost living at the big house, where she tried to explain her actions to her very sceptical grand parents. While they were no fans of family breakdown and divorce, they had never really been overly rapt in Angela, and had not been all that surprised when she left. Or that disappointed for that matter, except for the kids. Bill was better off without her, they thought.

As for Harry, well after being very suspicious for a start, they soon felt very comfortable with him, and grew to enjoy his company. He and Grandpa Douglas found many things to talk about, although Harry was careful to steer clear of politics, while he and Grandma enjoyed time in the kitchen swapping recipe ideas and cooking big meals for the five of them. When they left, they took with them one of her Christmas puddings and enough biscuits to last them for weeks.

They took something else with them too. Harry and Bill were making a bacon and egg breakfast on Boxing Day when an excited Cassie burst into the room.

"Harry," she said. "Come and see what I found."
He could hardly keep up with her as she led him to the barn, and then up a ladder to the loft.

"Look. Aren't they cute?" She fell to her knees and carefully picked up a squirming black kitten from the litter of four sharing a box with their mother. Watching her cuddle and stroke it, Harry thought to himself, she is only a little girl after all, not the grown up they all thought she had become. Meeting with her family had reinforced his commitment to look after her back in Brisbane. He was determined to do whatever he could to help her grow up in the absence of her parents. She was about to put his new resolution to its first test.

"Harry, do you think we could take him home with us? Please? Pretty please?"

He was charmed by her pleading smile and the look of absolute rapture on her pretty face.

"Of course we can Cassie, if you want to. Provided your father can spare one that is, but I've a sneaking suspicion that he will be only too happy to agree. Which one do you like?"

She held one out to him. "This one with the white feet. I'm going to call him Soxy. Want a nurse?"

So Soxy was soon to join his burgeoning household at Windsor. He could hardly believe his good fortune. From now on his house would become a home.

ॐ

"What a lovely man," Grandma said, as she waved at the retreating car. "He'll do a marvellous job of looking after Cassie, don't you think Bill?"

He put his arm around her and led her back to the big house. "Yes Mum. I'm sure he will," he said. "Not that she needs much help. She's a big girl now, almost a woman you might say and she seems to be doing a pretty good job of that herself don't you think? Now, how about a cup of tea, and maybe a biscuit, if there's any left in the house that is."

CHAPTER TWELVE

A lot had happened in Cassie's life before they reconvened at the farm for the following Christmas. For one thing it was the third trip out west for the year, including weekends to coincide with her birthday and the Roma show. She kept in regular touch with her father and her grandparents by phone and mail, and for the first time in many years, Bill came to Brisbane and stayed with them for Exhibition week. Harry's dreams had been realised. Father and daughter were back together.

He had less success however in his attempts to reconcile Cassie with her mother. Not so much less success, but actually no success. In spite of his repeated offers to take her to the Coast, she steadfastly refused to be convinced. Her life was now in order, and she was reluctant to risk her hard won independence. In spite of his constant nagging, the best he could achieve was a short letter every couple of months. He suspected they were rather brief and would not have disclosed too much about her current situation. As the new year dawned, he made a resolution to try even harder to organise a reconciliation.

The new year also brought a big change in her work-place. Craig had been promoted to the position of State Secretary of the Hospital Employees Union. Based in the city, he now had a staff of ten people, but was determined to make sure Cassie was one of them. She had completed a Diploma in Business Administration during the year, taught herself to type reasonably well, and her wage had increased accordingly. It was an easy decision to follow the man who had made it all possible for her where she became his personal assistant.

Cassie applied herself diligently to her new responsibilities, and as the year passed she became increasingly aware of an increasing attraction towards her boss. By necessity they worked closely together and she was even called on to handle a lot of his personal matters. This gave her an insight into his personality that was not evident to others who would have seen him as somewhat arrogant and very ambitious, but she saw a vulnerability that drove him to be brusque and aggressive in his dealings with everyone. Everyone but her, that is.

With her he was always patient, polite, and seemed infatuated by her. Even naive young Cassie picked up on it, sometimes feeling uncomfortable when she sensed him gazing at her as she worked. On one occasion he asked her if she had a boyfriend, and seemed surprised when she told him she had never thought about it. Her life revolved around her job, her study, and helping Harry to run his house. It never occurred to her that there might be anything more than mutual respect between them. After all, he was married.

"Craig," she called out through the open door, holding her hand over the phone. "It's Mrs Thomas again. Will I put her through?"

"No." Cassie was alarmed at the nastiness of his response as he hurried past her and left the office. "That silly woman knows not to ring me at work. Tell her I'm out and you don't know when I'll be back. I'll bring you a coffee." With that, he was gone.

Cassie tentatively conveyed his message to his wife and was sure she heard her sobbing as she hung up the phone. Obviously things were not going very well in the Thomas household. It was none of her business, but as the months went by, it was to become so.

The attention Craig was paying to Cassie increased to the point where he was taking her to lunch several times per week, and buying her little presents from time to time. When her birthday came he presented her with an expensive looking package. She opened it to find a gold pendant featuring a flashing opal, her birth stone.

"Craig! You shouldn't have," she cried. "It's beautiful, but you shouldn't have spent so much on me."

He beamed at her as she tried to hook it up behind her neck. "Rubbish," he chuckled. "You're worth it. Here, let me help." He stepped behind her, fastened the clasp, and smoothed it down with his finger. Then, leaning forward, he placed a gentle kiss on her neck. "Happy birthday Cas," he whispered in her ear.

Her face flushed and she gasped at his touch. Craig placed his hands on her shoulders and gently turned her to face him. She looked up into his face which was wracked with desire, while a smile played around his lips. Those sensuous lips. "Thanks Craig," she whispered, and then, hardly knowing what she was doing, reached up to meet them.

❦

Behind the closed door of his office their little romance was played out over the following weeks. Cassie worried incessantly about what was happening, particularly because of Craig's marriage, but he wouldn't listen to her concerns.

"Don't be silly Cas," he said, holding her in his arms. "She'll never know, and probably wouldn't care much anyway. We've not been getting on too well lately, as you know full well. Besides, what goes on in the office stays in the office eh?"

Heading towards Christmas that is precisely all that had happened. Fully aware of her inexperience, Craig was careful not to push her past her comfort zone. An occasional dinner together, constant flirting, and some stolen moments of passion in his office was as far as they went. Cassie forced herself to put his wife out of her mind. What they were doing need not threaten the marriage. It was just a bit of fun, for both of them. It would blow over in time. But fate and Craig's ambition intervened.

Always on the lookout for ways to promote himself and progress his position in the Union movement, he now had aspirations of running for National Secretary.

"Just think of it Cas. We could double our salaries if I could snag that job. There would be all sorts of perks too," he said smiling seductively at her. "Overseas trips even, and I would need to take my personal assistant with me wouldn't I?"

"Craig! Don't be awful," she replied laughingly. "You would have to take Mrs Thomas with you, not me. I'd have to stay here and protect your back so you still had your job when you came back."

All the humour had drained from his face, and he became deadly serious.

"Cassie, if I did get the National job I would have to move to Sydney to live. I wouldn't be taking Debra with me. For one thing, she wouldn't be prepared to leave her family in Brisbane. She spends more time running after them than she does looking after me, that's for sure. Her mother has dementia you see."

"I'm sorry," Cassie said. "It must be awful for her."

"And me," he said bitterly. "She's not the woman I married."

Cassie tried to hide her embarrassment by busying herself

with the papers on her desk. She felt his presence behind her before he placed his hands gently on her shoulders. As usual, his touch sent a shiver through her body. She knew this was wrong and she should tell him to stop doing it, but the words always froze in her throat. She sat, mesmerised, as he started to massage her tense muscles.

"There is another reason why I wouldn't take her with me Cas," he almost whispered to her. "I want to be with you, not her."

"No Craig. You can't. We can't. You know that." Eyes shut, hands in her lap, she found she could scarcely breathe.

"Shush. Relax." He stepped back, alarmed at the thought that he might have pushed his advances too far. "Let's just see what happens eh? In the mean time, I need you to make arrangements for next week's National Conference in Melbourne. You know, flights, car hire, and hotel bookings, and Cassie, I'd like you to come with me. I'll need your help down there. Everyone brings their PA's."

With that, he disappeared into his office, leaving Cassie shaken and nervous, but the more she thought about what he had said, the more excited she became. A trip to Melbourne on a plane. She had never flown before, and the conference was at a top hotel too, in the city centre. As she set about her given task, she put Craig's advances out of her mind. He was probably only being silly anyway. He'd never leave his wife. He was just a tease. She could handle him.

❦

She could hardly wait to tell Harry all about her up-coming adventure. He would be so proud of her. Here she was less than two years into the job, earning good money, and already indispensable to her boss. Time to worry about Craig's plan to move to Sydney when it eventuated, if it ever did. She met him at the top of the steps.

"Guess what Harry?"

"Soxy caught another mouse?"

"No," she laughed. "Nothing like that. He's too fat and lazy anyway. No. This has to do with work."

Harry dropped his lunch box on the sink and turned to face her.

"Well by the look on your face, it can't be that you've got the sack," he joked.

"Just the opposite actually. Craig and I are going to the Union's National Convention in MELBOURNE, no less," she gushed. "He needs me there to help him handle all the paper work so he can concentrate on lobbying for the National Secretary's position. Isn't it exciting?"

Excitement wasn't how Harry viewed the news. While Cassie had never let on to him about the clandestine little affair that had been going on in the office, he had noticed how she clammed up whenever Craig's name came up in conversation, and he was aware of him having a bit of a reputation as a lady's man when he had been based at the hospital. Surely there wasn't something going on between them was there? But you never know, he decided. Cassie had certainly grown into an attractive young woman over the last twelve months, but still a very naive one who was more likely to play around with her cat than a man. Still. Perhaps he should warn her. She was waiting for his answer, a searching look on her face.

"Aren't you happy for me? We'll be away for two nights

Harry, and we're staying at the Grand Hyatt right in the centre of Melbourne."

Harry chuckled. "That'd be right. Nothing but the best for the Union hierarchy. Pity about us poor old workers who front up with our fees to pay the bills." He gave her a friendly hug. "Of course I'm happy for you Cas. You've worked hard and you deserve it."

"But?" she asked, noticing his less than enthusiastic expression.

"Well, to be honest, I would worry a bit about you two going away together on your own. He's a married man you know, and people might talk."

Cassie couldn't hide the flush that she felt rise to her cheeks. Surely Harry didn't suspect anything did he? She tried to laugh it off.

"Don't be silly," she said, giving him a playful slap on the arm. "He's my boss, and I'm just his flunky assistant, that's all. Besides, all the other delegates will be bringing their PA's too. We'll hardly be alone, as you put it. Don't you worry about me." Then, giving him one of her broadest smiles, she added, "now, you're the cook, and I'm the dish-washer, so what's for dinner?"

Together they set about the evening chores, chatting happily. But Harry did worry. He worried a lot, because in the absence of her real family, he had grown to consider her his responsibility, and there was something about Craig Thomas that left him feeling uneasy. He couldn't quite put his finger on what he felt, and maybe it was nothing. Perhaps he was just being over protective of her. Just like I would with the daughter I never had, he thought with a wry grin to himself.

But he couldn't bring himself to rain on her parade. She was so excited about the trip, and really, what could possibly go wrong? They would be part of a large group of people staying in a posh hotel, and it was only for two days. He decided to put his concerns out of his mind and help her to enjoy the moment. He dug into his wallet for some cash.

"Merry Christmas," he said, handing her a crisp one hundred dollar note. "This is my early Christmas present for you in case you need to buy a bit of good gear for your trip. We can't let those Southerners put it over us Queenslanders can we now? You buy yourself something nice Cas and make your boss proud."

"Harry!" she squealed, flinging her arms around him and planting a kiss on his cheek. "You shouldn't have. It's too much, but thank you, thank you, thank you. You're so good to me. I don't know how I can ever repay you."

Harry chuckled as he gave her a friendly pat on the shoulder. "You already have Cassie. Every day. You've made my boring old life worth living again. It is I who owe you so much." Then, in a serious tone he added, "just you make sure you look after yourself down there, won't you?"

"Of course I will," she replied "and I'll have Craig there to look after me."

That's what worries me he thought, but didn't say.

※

The plane trip was an exciting new experience for her. Terrified at take-off, she soon relaxed and gasped as they passed through fluffy white clouds as they rose over Moreton Bay. She gazed out of the window for practically the whole trip while Craig worked on the paper he was presenting at the conference. Soon she found herself immersed in the opulence of the Grand Hyatt. Her room sported the biggest bed she had ever seen, gold taps in the bathroom, a refrigerator full of drinks, and a bowl of fruit on the coffee table. The wardrobe even had a fresh white gown on a hanger. Throwing open the curtains she looked out over the sprawling city from the tenth floor. Wow! This is the life she thought.

The conference itself also proved to be amazing. Two hundred delegates and support staff from all over Australia were seated around tables in the convention room, while the senior officials were ranged behind a long table on the stage. Reports, discussions and agenda items were presented and debated all day and long into the night, only to resume the next morning. Craig left Cassie to her own devices quite a bit as he campaigned amongst the delegates for the National Secretary's job he was after. Although she was undoubtedly the youngest person in the room, she found she was able to mix and socialise with the other attendees.

It all wound up with the Conference Dinner on Friday night. Cassie was stunning in her new royal blue off the shoulder dress she had bought with Harry's money, while her opal pendant sparkled at her throat. Craig proudly introduced her to all the important people in the room. Finally the night came to a close and they found themselves in the lift heading for the tenth floor. He put his arm around her shoulders and squeezed her gently.

"Thank you Cassie. You were brilliant. Far and away the most beautiful girl in the room, and you charmed the pants off all those old buffers."

"Don't be silly. I'm sure they all thought I was just a starry eyed schoolgirl, totally out of place, but I did enjoy myself.

Thank you so much for bringing me." She reached up to give him a peck on the cheek, but he pulled her to him and kissed her deeply. They sprang apart as the doors opened on their floor, but they were alone as they headed hand in hand along the passage.

"It's been such a wonderful night," Cassie said. "I wish it would never end."

"Well I can't organise that I'm afraid," Craig chuckled, "but I can make it last a little longer. Would you like to come into my room for a nightcap? I've got half a bottle of nice red in there to get rid of before we go tomorrow. It would be a shame to waste it."

"Ooh Craig. I shouldn't. I've already drunk more tonight than I have in the rest of my life. I'm feeling quite tipsy in fact," she giggled.

"One more won't hurt you Cas, and you only have to stagger next door to be home. I'll walk you there."

She felt excited, even a little scared, as she followed him into his room. While they had snuck in plenty of secret petting sessions in his office, and even in public places when no-one was around, this was the first time they were really alone to-gether.

"Make yourself at home Cas," he ordered. "I'll get that drink."

She looked around the room and was struck by the manliness of it. His clothes lay draped over chairs, papers covered the table in a total mess, and shoes and socks were scattered over the floor. Above all, she was aware of the manly deodorant to which she had become accustomed in the office. She kicked off her high-heeled shoes that were killing her and sank into the plush leather lounge chair.

"Here we are," he said, handing her a glass of red wine. "I hope you like it. Let's drink a toast."

"What to?"

Craig's eyes smouldered with desire that Cassie couldn't fail to notice. "To us Cas," he replied in a husky voice. "To you and me, and our future." They clinked glasses and, looking into each other's eyes, drank deeply, then Craig sat their glasses on the coffee table, and wrapped her in his arms.

An hour later the bottle was empty, and Cassie was feeling quite strange.

"I'd better go" she said as she started to stand up, but flopped back into the chair, landing on his lap. "Oops!" she giggled. "Sorry. I think I've had one too many. Help me up will you boss. I must go home."

Craig pulled her to him. "You don't have to Cas," he said huskily, looking steadily into her eyes. "You're welcome to stay."

Confused emotions coursed through her. While her heart would have agreed in an instant, her mind held her back. She knew what they had been doing was wrong, but up till now it was relatively harmless. The memory of Craig's wife sobbing on the phone sprang to her mind and she suddenly felt ashamed of herself.

"No. No. It's wrong. I've got to go." She struggled to her feet and took a few steps towards the door before she passed out and dropped to the floor.

ক

Through the hazy realms of sleep Cassie's dreams drifted through waves of emotions. Fear and disgust mixed with elation and excitement that befuddled her mind. Cassie's eyes sprang open as she realised something was touching her. Craig's hand lay across her naked stomach. Resisting the impulse to fling it aside and spring to her feet, she turned her head slowly and observed his sleeping form beside her. Then she focussed on her surroundings. They were in his room, in his bed in fact. Slowly at first, memories of the previous night returned.

What had she done? She couldn't remember anything after she got up to leave. How did she end up like this? Carefully, she lifted the sheet and peeked under it. They were both naked. She was shocked. What had she done? Or rather, what had he done, because she could recall nothing? Then realisation dawned as she registered a dull ache in her groin. My God, she thought. He raped me!

She sprang to her feet and had to steady herself on the bedhead as dizziness again over-came her.

"Cassie. What's up with you?" Craig also clambered off the bed and came to help her.

"Don't touch me!" she shouted at him, cringing away from his advance. "What did you do to me?"

He held up his hands in submission and backed off. "Steady on there Cas," he said. "What do you mean, what did I do to you? We had a few drinks and then you agreed to sleep with me. Remember?"

"No, I do NOT remember any such thing," she snarled, snatching up a pillow and holding it in front of herself. "You raped me Craig. How could you do it?"

The blood drained from his face as her accusation hit home. "Hey, steady on Cas. I did no such thing. Maybe you can't remember now, and maybe you had a bit too much to drink, but you agreed last night. I didn't force you to do anything you didn't want to." A strained smile broke across his face. "You enjoyed it too Cassie. You told me so often enough." He held out a hand towards her. "Now come on. Don't get all prudish with me."

They stared wordlessly at each other until she finally said in a steady voice that broached no argument, "Go into the bathroom Craig. I want to get dressed."

When he tentatively peeked back into the room a few minutes later it was empty.

⁂

Back in her own room, Cassie fell onto her bed and sobbed silently into her pillow. After a while her thoughts turned from last night to consider the situation. Here she was, stranded in Melbourne, with no option other than to return to Brisbane with Craig. As to whether she could continue to work for him, that was a question for later on. Maybe she had agreed to his suggestion as he claimed, but she couldn't bring herself to believe that she had, even though she had probably been drunk. Above all else, she would have been too scared, just like she had been on the street all those months ago.

She placed a call to his room and told him she would be ready to leave for the airport in half an hour. Then she spent most of that scrubbing the previous night from her body in the shower. It proved to be a long and strained trip back to Queensland.

CHAPTER THIRTEEN

By the time she faced Craig at work on Monday morning Cassie had made up her mind how to handle the situation. Try as she might to remember what had happened in Melbourne, her mind was blank. Maybe it had been her fault. After all, she had gone into his room, and their sessions together had been getting pretty torrid recently. What could she expect would happen? All it took was a few glasses of wine to lower her inhibitions and she could hardly blame Craig for taking advantage of the situation. She felt she had no option but to accept responsibility and move on, hoping they could still work together.

When Craig came into the office she was already hard at work. He breathed a sigh of relief as he walked past her and headed towards his room. Once there, he flopped into his chair and re-lived last week's events once more. He had thought of little else since he had put Cassie in a cab at the airport on Saturday morning. The plane trip had been a nightmare with hardly a word passing between them. Discretion seemed to be the best tactic he decided, and Cassie seemed to be reluctant to talk at all. Neither of them mentioned the previous night and she had been driven off without even a civil goodbye.

Like her, he had spent hours wondering how they would fare working together from now on. Perhaps he should let her go, but that would hardly be fair. It wasn't her fault. He was the adult, and he had taken advantage of the situation. Who would have guessed she would react like she had? Now he had to live with the risk that Debra would find out, and he couldn't afford to let that happen. It would ruin his career. He reached for the phone and asked her to come in.

Cassie stood in front of his desk, avoiding his eyes, and clasping her notebook in front of her.

"Craig, I..."

"No Cas," he interrupted. "Let me have my say first. Come and sit down."

They sat as far apart as the divan allowed and he reached over to lift her chin. "Cassie, look at me." She did. "Cassie, from the bottom of my heart I want to apologise to you. I should never have let that happen between us. It was my fault. I should have seen it coming and controlled myself. I'm so sorry, and I want your forgiveness. Please."

A tear rolled slowly down her cheek and she wiped it away with the back of her hand. Craig tried to put his arm round her but she shrugged it off. Eventually, she spoke.

"I'm not sure what happened Craig, because I can't remember, but it was at least partly my fault. It has been all along. I should never have let us become involved like we have in here. You're a married man for God's sake. Does your poor wife know?"

"Of course not," he snorted.

"Well you can rest assured on two counts Craig. She won't hear about it from me." She caught his almost imperceptible sigh of relief.

"And the second?"

"It won't happen again. Any of it, here or anywhere else. If you still want me to work for you that is."

He looked abashed and disappointed, as well as relieved, as he sank back in the chair.

"Of course I do. I couldn't run this place without you." He gave her a nervous smile and extended his hand. "Just business from now on. Deal?"

Cassie gave his hand a shake. "Deal," she said, and rose to go.

As she left his office she didn't turn as he called after her.

"Thanks Cassie. I really appreciate your decision."

What ever did he mean by that she wondered? Did he have a guilty conscience perhaps? If only she could remember what happened. Surely she couldn't have been that drunk. Frowning, she returned to her desk.

❧

The following week she and Harry went to Roma for Christmas. If anyone noticed a change in her, no-one said anything, although she noticed Harry looking at her in a funny way a few times. Gone was her usual effervescent self, replaced by a more mature and serious disposition that seemed to him to have only been present since her Melbourne trip. Even when telling him all about it she didn't seem as excited as he would have expected. Maybe Craig hadn't looked after as well as he should have, but every time he tried to ask about him she clammed up and changed the subject.

By the time they returned after the Christmas break she was even more silent and unhappy. Her period was over-due. She tried hard to convince herself that it might just be due to her first sexual encounter and would sort itself out. Then, two weeks after she returned to work, she threw up her breakfast one morning. And again the next morning. She now knew for certain, and she was terrified. What on earth should she do? Obviously, she had to tell Craig.

"I'm pregnant."

The blood drained from his face as he rocked back in his chair. She stood in front of his desk clasping her hands in front of her.

"You can't be," he almost whispered. "Are you sure?"

"Sure enough, but I haven't had a test yet. I thought you should know first."

"What are you going to do?"

"What are WE going to do you mean Craig? Don't forget your role in this, but to answer your question, I don't know."

His attitude didn't surprise her. It was just what she had expected. The experience had changed her opinion of her boss. No longer was she the starry eyed sixteen year old recruit who was so impressed by him. She now saw him for what he was, an ambitious, devious go-getter who would do whatever it took to achieve his goals. This accident was just another impediment to his future success that had to be removed. His expression was severe as he weighed up the situation.

"You're going to have to get rid of it Cassie," he said. "You know that, don't you?"

She didn't answer him, but continued to stare him down.

"I'll help you make the arrangements, and pay the bills, but you can't possibly have this baby."

Her voice when she answered rasped with cynicism, and she saw it hit home.

"Why not Craig? What's it to you? Afraid Debra would find out aren't you? You don't care about me at all."

"Don't be silly Cas. Of course I do. You know that, but we

have to be reasonable. It's not in either of our interests, so let me make the arrangements, please?"

"I'll think about it," she snapped. "Can I get back to work now?"

Taking up a pen, his attention returned to his work. Without a trace of irony he said, "Of course. Take care."

Cassie fled from the room.

As he left the office later on he handed her an envelope. "This is a letter of introduction to a friend of mine Cassie. His address and phone number is inside. He'll take care of you and I'll fix him up. Oh, and take the rest of the week off. I'll see you next Monday." With that he left before she could reply.

Cassie was stunned at his off-hand callousness. Was this the same man who had seemed to be so loving towards her? Take care of me indeed, she thought. Kill my baby is what he means, the bastard. Worse than that. Our baby. How could he be so thoughtless and cruel? She packed up her desk, grabbed her bag, and in a semi daze headed home. Telling Harry was not going to be easy, but he would have to know.

*

That night she told him. Naturally he was shocked at first, then angry, and finally worried. His doubts about her trip to Melbourne sprang to his mind, but in his wildest dreams he had never thought something like this would happen. The fact that Cassie couldn't remember how it had come about heightened his anger. Fancy that mongrel taking advantage of an innocent young kid like Cassie, especially when he was a married man. Getting her so drunk that she passed out, and then virtually raping her. No, not virtually, he decided. If she couldn't remember it happening, then it was rape, pure and simple.

Cassie was sitting staring into space on the lounge. He sat next to her and put his arm around her shoulders.

"What are you going to do love?" he asked quietly.

He felt her shoulders shrug. They sat silently, the only sound coming from Soxy's purring where he slept in her lap.

"You should report the bastard to the police. You know that, don't you?"

"No Harry. I can't do that. I can't help feeling it was partly my fault, maybe even all my fault. I shouldn't have led him on. It's been going on for months you know. I guess we both got carried away, what with the wine and all."

Several questions came to his mind and he wondered if she was also considering them. The first was a tough decision for a girl like her to make on her own under any circumstances, and she only had days to make it. In many ways it would simplify matters for both of them if she agreed to have an abortion, but even an old bachelor like him realised how hard that would be for her. It might be something she regretted for the rest of her life. On the other hand, how on earth could she handle having the baby and then looking after it as a single young girl, alone in the big city?

"Are you going to do what he says Cas?"

He felt her shoulders shake as she started to sob silently. He held her till she stopped and turned to look at him through bleary eyes.

"I don't think I can Harry," she whispered. "I just don't think I can."

Her answer didn't surprise him, but it did worry him. Feeling responsible for her as he now did, he wondered if he could support her through all that she would face. It was now time to ask the second question on his mind.

"Will you tell your mother?"

"No way!" she almost screamed, as she pulled away from him and jumped to her feet. "Under no circumstances. I know exactly what her reaction would be. You must promise me Harry. You won't tell her, will you?"

In spite of the tension, he chuckled as he patted the seat beside him. "Don't be silly Cas. I wouldn't do that if you didn't want me to." He patted the seat again. "Now come on. Sit down and we'll see what we can work out. Firstly, I'll do what I can to help you, no matter what you decide to do. You can count on that for starters. Okay?"

She sank back onto the lounge. "Thanks Harry," was all she said, so he continued.

"As I said, I'll do what I can, but that won't be enough you know. We'll need help, and if not your mother, then who else can you count on?" Harry knew the answer, but he wanted her to come up with her own answers. That way she would be more committed to make it work. Eventually she spoke the words he wanted her to say.

"I suppose I'll have to tell Dad," she Mumbled. "He'll understand better than Mum, and I know he wouldn't want me to have an abortion, that's for sure. Will you help me do that?"

Again he chuckled, trying desperately to cheer her up. "I'll take a couple of days off work and we can go out and tell him together eh? If I know your father Cassie, and I think I do by now, I reckon he just might be tickled pink at being asked to help. I know he feels partly responsible for you running away from school, and this could give him the chance to make it up to you."

"Do you really think so?" she asked tentatively.

"I don't think so. I know so," he said. "Now, how about a nice cup of tea for me and hot chocolate for you eh? I'll make it. You wash up."

For the first time that night, she smiled.

On Monday morning Craig glanced at her in surprise, then walked straight past and entered his office. Cassie waited a couple of minutes, then followed, tapped on the door, and without waiting to be invited, went in and stood in front of the desk.

"Cassie," he said. "I wasn't expecting you in today. "How are you? Come and sit down," he added, coming around his desk and motioning her towards the divan.

"I'd rather stand thanks Craig," she said stiffly.

He sat on the edge of his desk. "Okay. If you prefer." The look on her face sent a shiver up his spine. "Why are you here Cassie? I told you to take the week off to arrange....you know, to see my friend."

Her steely eyes stared into his. "I'm not going Craig. I can't do it."

The blood drained from his face. He stood to face her and reached for her hands, but she took a step back.

"What? But Cassie you must. Don't you see? It's the only solution to your problem."

"To OUR problem Craig," she rasped. "It may be your solution, but it's not the only solution, as you so lovingly call it. I'm going to have this baby, whether you like it or not."

He was distraught. "But how will you support it for God's

117

sake? You're only a girl, and on your own."

After planning this encounter all weekend Cassie was well prepared for his reaction. It was just what she expected. No responsibility on his part, and sweep it under the carpet. Well that wasn't going to happen. Over a long Sunday breakfast, she and Harry had worked out a strategy for handling the man for whom they now had no respect at all.

"I'll work here as long as I can, and then use child-care after it's born." The look of abject horror that appeared on his face didn't surprise her either. She pressed on. "Oh, and Craig, as the father, I expect you will want access in return for paternal support."

He slumped back onto the desk. "But Cassie, you can't be serious. You can't work in here when you're obviously pregnant. Think what the staff would say."

"Yes Craig. I know what they'd say, and they'd be right wouldn't they? I wouldn't have to tell them who the father was."

By now Cassie was in full flight and taking delight in the distraught character in front of her. He deserved it. She just wished Harry had been here to see how well she handled him, and she wasn't finished yet either.

"Would you tell Debra?"

"I wouldn't have to. You would. How else could you explain the paternity payments going out of your account?"

"What paternity payments? You're not trying to blackmail me are you?"

"Not at all Craig, but you wouldn't expect me to raise OUR baby on my own would you? Think about it Daddy. On Friday you offered your solution. Today I'm offering you mine. The big difference is, I have the law on my side."

With that, she flounced out of his office, leaving him gaping open-mouthed after her.

❧

An hour later, he buzzed her on the inter-office line and curtly ordered her to come into his office. Stage two she thought, and after taking a few deep breaths, she walked in without knocking, closing the door behind her. She saw immediately that he was back to his usual domineering self. No invitation to sit down this time. He left her standing as he lounged in his chair.

"Okay Cassie. Here's the deal." She steeled herself for the out-burst, but he went on in a level, businesslike voice. She waited nervously.

"Point one. If you cause trouble for me over this I will deny everything and hang you out to dry. I can find someone to say they saw you flirting with one of the young fellows at Melbourne. You were quite the centre of attention, and no-one saw you with me very much.

Point two. If Debra hears about this, all bets are off. Again, I'll deny everything, and she'll take my word over yours. I can guarantee that.

Point three. If you play ball, I'll keep you on the Union pay-roll for six months. All Unions have phantom employees, normally going into their own leader's pockets. Again, it stops the day you cause trouble.

Point four. After the baby is born, I am prepared to make a one off payment of five thousand dollars in return for a signed agreement that you have not cited me as the father, and that you will make no further claims against me in the future.

Have I made myself clear?" He was back in control, not quite

119

smug, but certainly confident and self assured. She was sure he meant every word he said, and a chill ran up her spine as she considered the prospects of making an enemy of him. His cold blue eyes never left her face.

Cassie stared him down, waited a few seconds, and in the strongest voice she could muster said, "Clear as crystal. Can I go now?"

He waved towards the door, reached for the phone, and started dialling a number. Cassie closed the door quietly behind her, picked up her bag, and left the office without a word to anyone.

❧

Harry had been right in judging her father's reaction. Unlike Craig, he accepted responsibility for what he saw as his part in the whole sorry saga that had led to his little girl arriving home in this predicament. They all agreed it would be best for Cassie to stay in Brisbane for her pregnancy where she would be closer to doctors and hospitals than on the property outside Roma, and Harry was only too pleased to have her there.

Bill went with Cassie to the big house to break the news to his parents that they were to become great grandparents. Their excitement was clearly tempered by the circumstances, and their preference would have been for a grand garden wedding in the grounds, followed after the appropriate time by the baby, but they loved Cassie enough to hide their feelings from her. No doubt, when the time came, they would accept him or her into the family fold without question.

On the return trip to Brisbane, it was hard to say who was purring the loudest, Soxy sitting in Cassie's lap, or Harry behind the wheel thinking of becoming a de-facto grandfather for the first, and most likely last time. For her part, Cassie was just pleased everything had been sorted out. Now she could settle down to planning for her baby's arrival. In time, Craig Thomas would become just a bad dream, and she would never set eyes on him again, or so she thought.

CHAPTER FOURTEEN

True to Craig's word, her usual wage appeared as if by magic in Cassie's account each fortnight. At first it worried her to think that it was actually being stolen from the Union, but she assuaged her conscience with the thought that there were probably many more illegal perks going into the pockets of Craig and his Union buddies than her phantom wage.

The fortunate outcome for her was that she didn't have to find another job, which was just as well as for some weeks her days were plagued with morning sickness. When that passed, she experienced a feeling of contentment and well-being that she had never known before in her life. She was struck by the certainty that her decision to keep her baby was the right one, and she shuddered every time she recalled Craig's assumption that she would want an abortion. Even the thought of it disgusted her. You poor little thing, she thought, as she stroked her slowly growing belly.

Harry was absolutely marvellous with her, fussing after her when she was sick, and cheering her up when she felt low. He introduced her to his own long-standing doctor, and drove her to ante-natal clinics. Now, as he saw how well and happy she had become, he made a suggestion to her, one which she happily adopted. She signed on for a twelve week cooking course at TAFE, and was soon serving up dishes far more interesting than Harry's bachelor inspired fare.

As well as a handsome diploma, the course also provided her with something else missing in her life, some social interaction. Like her, most of the other students were youngsters learning to fend for themselves while living away from home. Cassie made friends with them easily, but it was one of the lecturers that caught most of her interest.

Bradley Harcourt worked in the bistro of a city hotel but still found time to lecture three nights per week. For some reason, he and Cassie hit it off from day one, and by the time the course came to a close, they were great friends. He was twenty four. What is it about me Cassie wondered, that I seem to be attracted to older men. Maybe the torturous path she had chosen to take in life had forced her grow up quicker than normal, and approaching motherhood could only have added to that maturity. For whatever reason, she found herself increasingly attracted to him, and when he no longer saw her at TAFE he started calling on her at home.

In his private thoughts, Harry was not totally impressed with the man. Six years older than Cassie, he seemed to lack the stable attitude to life that his age should have dictated. He had changed jobs constantly since he started work, and seemed to be infatuated with the idea of travelling the world for years before settling down. Hardly the credentials for a long term relationship with a heavily pregnant young mum-to-be, he thought. But in true Harry fashion, he kept his thoughts to himself as he watched the growing friendship between the two of them.

❦

One other concern was playing on Harry's mind too. That was the fact that so far, Cassie hadn't told her mother of her situation, and he thought she should. In spite of many hints thrown at her, she had stubbornly refused to do anything about it. Finally, as the months passed, and her due date approached, he decided it was time for more direct action. After finishing the washing up, which was now his job since Cassie did the cooking these days, he joined her in front of the telly.

"What's on love?" he asked. "Something interesting?"

"No, not really," she replied. "David Attenborough's wild life show. Soxy likes it, probably because of all the birds on it. Do you want to watch something else?"

Harry reached for the remote and turned it off. "No," he ventured cautiously. "There's something I want to talk to you about. Do you mind?"

"Of course not. You sound very serious though Harry. Is something wrong," she asked anxiously.

"No, no. Of course not," he chuckled, easing the tension. He paused, then said, "It's about your mother." He watched the anticipated look of apprehension cross her face, but she said nothing, so he continued. "I think you should tell her about your baby Cas. No, I don't think you should. I know you should," he added. Still she said nothing, as she considered what she knew to be his view. Why was it that the thought held such terror for her she wondered. There was no way she could be sent back to school now, and her mother certainly wouldn't want Cassie and her baby to live with her and Aldo. The thought made her shudder. Harry noticed.

"I'm sorry love," he said simply. "I don't want to upset you, but I just think she has a right to know. Even if you wrote and told her it would be better than nothing, but I wish you'd go to see her. Just once, and I'd come with you, just like I did with your dad. That worked out okay. Even your grandies are thrilled so he tells me. Maybe your mother would be too."

Harry waited patiently while she sat pondering his suggestion. He recognised the emotional battle going on in her head, and at the same time, in her heart. She had never forgiven her mother for breaking up her family, and it seemed unlikely that she ever would, but she was still her mother after all. There must be some residual maternal feelings in her heart he thought hopefully. When he noticed tears welling to her eyes, he knew he was right, and put his arm around her.

"Come on Cas," he said. "Let me ring her and ask if we can come down on Sunday eh? If things get out of hand we'll jump in the car and come home, but at least you will know you did the right thing by her. And yourself," he added.

Without a word, she rose and went to her room, returning a minute later with a phone number written on a scrap of paper and handed it to Harry.

"I couldn't even remember her number," she said, somewhat ashamedly. "I had to look it up." Then, sitting beside him again, she gave him a peck on the cheek. "Thanks Harry. You're right again, I know, and I'll do my best to make it up with her, but be warned, it might prove a lot harder than you think."

He gave her shoulder a squeeze as he headed for his office. "It'll be okay Cas. Trust me. I won't let anything bad happen to you. I promise." She did trust him, implicitly, but was still terrified at the thought of confronting her mother and Aldo.

❧

The door was tentatively opened by a woman who remained half hidden behind it.

Cassie stepped forward, confusion etched in her face. "Mum? Is that you?" she asked. From behind the door appeared a person she could barely recognise as her mother. Dressed in a baggy track-suit and slippers, straggly hair hanging limply to her shoulders, and with no make-up on her puffy tired looking face, she was nothing like the image Cassie had retained of her mother the last time she had seen her at parent's day. She was a wreck, and Cassie couldn't hold back the involuntary gasp that escaped her.

Angela's gaze shifted from Cassie's face to her almost full term belly and she let out a scream. "Cassandra! No, no, no. Don't tell me. It can't be you." With that she turned and ran sobbing into the unit. Harry stepped forward and put his arm around Cassie.

"Come on love," he said encouragingly. "We can't leave now. She'll calm down if we give her a chance."

Together they went to where Angela sat hunched over on a sofa, her head in her hands, her shoulders wreaked by audible sobs. Harry nodded at Cassie. She cautiously went forward and sat beside her mother, putting an arm around her and sitting patiently until her sobbing stopped and she raised her tear-stained eyes to look at her daughter. Once again, her gaze settled on the bulging body beside her. She seemed to be speechless.

"Are you alright Mum? Cassie asked. "You don't look well. Are you sick?"

Angela straightened herself and wiped the back of her hand across her eyes as she struggled to take control of herself. "I'm sorry Cassandra," she blurted out. "I don't know what came over me. It's probably just that....well I haven't heard from you, and I didn't know....you know," she stammered, nodding at Cassie's obvious state of pregnancy.

Suddenly she remembered a second person had stood at the front door. Her gaze swung around to take in Harry, standing hat in hand at the back of the room. Her mouth fell open. "My God," she exclaimed. "Are you the father?"

In spite of the circumstances, Cassie smiled as she stood and motioned to him to come over. "No Mum," she said. "He's better than the father. This is my good friend and life saver Harry Elliott. He rang you to arrange our visit. Remember?"

Angela was struggling to regain her composure. "Oh of course. I'm terribly sorry mister Elliott. How rude of me. Please come and sit down. Can I take your hat? And Cassandra, you take that comfortable chair over there. I'll be back in a minute," she gushed as she fled from the room.

Harry handed her his hat and sat where directed. Although her appearance didn't measure up against Cassie's description, he recognised in her demeanour the social butterfly that had so upset her more introverted daughter. Still, she wasn't all bad, and things could have gone worse than they had so far. Maybe he could forge a reconciliation with her like he had with Bill. He hoped so. It wasn't right for families to be torn apart like this. He raised his eyebrows at Cassie.

She shrugged her shoulders in reply. Her mother seemed pretty weird to her, not at all like the tarted up floosie she had been the last time she saw her. No make up, shabby clothes. It wasn't like the mother she had come to know since they left the farm and moved to the Gold Coast. I wonder what playboy Aldo thinks of her. Maybe she's changed back to the way she had been. But when she floated back into the room, she was back to normal. Smart dress, mid heel shoes, make-up, and hair pushed into a chignon on her head. The old Angela was back.

"I'm so sorry to have been so rude to you both," she purred.

"It was inexcusable of me. Here's Cassandra whom I haven't seen for so long, and you've been good enough to drive her here Mr Elliott. I really do apologise for my rudeness. Now let me see. I must get us some refreshments. You must both be exhausted after your trip, and you must be famished Cassandra." Again her eyes fell to the all-too-obvious stomach. "You stay here and I'll just....."

Cassie could take it no longer. "Mum, for heaven's sake, stop fussing around and sit down will you?" she interrupted. "We came here to talk, and you haven't let us get a word in yet. For starters, this is Harry, not Mr Elliott, and as you know, I prefer Cassie these days."

Angela's mouth opened to protest, but Cassie continued. "Secondly, you can stop looking with such disdain at my stomach. Yes, I'm having a baby, and yes, I should have told you earlier, but I just wasn't game I suppose, because you see, the father is long gone, so there."

Silence followed as all three absorbed the tension in the room. It was broken by Angela. "Don't be like that Cassan...Cassie. I'm just worried about you. That's all. You don't have to tell me about it if you don't want to. I understand these things happen sometimes, but the last time I saw you, you were still a schoolgirl. It's hard for me to believe you're all grown up now."

The mention of school caused Cassie to glance nervously at her watch. "Where's Aldo Mum? Will he be home soon?"

Angela gave a bitter little laugh. "That's one thing you don't have to worry about dear. Like your man, he's long gone too. He left me for some-one years younger than him. Can you believe that?"

The incongruity of the situation seemed to be lost on her, but it brought a satisfied smile to Cassie's lips. "Well at last we have something in common Mum. We're both spurned women. Why don't you tell me what happened, and then I'll tell you my story." Harry sat quietly to one side as mother and daughter related their lives since that fateful day at school more than three years before.

Aldo had eventually tired of Angela and moved onto greener, and younger, pastures, packing his bags and moving out while Angela and Cameron were enjoying a holiday in Thailand. She never saw him, or even heard from him again. As for Cameron, he had never come back from their trip, and was living the life of a back-packer somewhere in South East Asia, but was due back soon. With no Aldo to support her, Angela had taken a job as a hostess in a nightclub, but appeared to Harry to be fragile and unhappy.

When it was her turn to speak Harry wondered if Cassie would reveal all of her secrets. With the exception of the night she met him on the street in the Valley, that is. The pride in her achievements showed through, from finding work, to gaining her certificate in business, and even in the friendship she had developed with him. She did admit that they had returned to the farm and become friendly with her father years ago, an admission that brought tears to her mother's eyes. Tears of anger perhaps, or resentment, or possibly even regret. Surely she must wish she had never left, he thought.

"So there you have it Mum," Cassie concluded. "My life since school."

Her speech had left Angela dumb-struck. She had no idea what she had expected had become of her daughter. Other than the call from that woman years ago to say she was safe and well

129

and those few terse little notes she had received since from Cassie, she had no idea what she had been up to all that time. Looking at her now, grown from schoolgirl into a young woman on her own, she felt ashamed for her role in causing the run-away.

"I did try to find you, you know," she said softly, "but other than the fact you were in Brisbane we didn't know where to start looking. Aldo was marvellous. We even reported you to the police, but as you were sixteen by then and had told us you were alright, there was nothing they could do."

Cassie was starting to feel sorry for the broken woman before them. Perhaps she should have come to see her earlier, but fear of rejection had held her back. Now the gulf between them had widened through separation and the simple fact that she was no longer the school-girl daughter she had been, and, on the other hand, Angela was no longer the loving devoted mother who she had been during her childhood.

"I'm sorry Mum," she mumbled.

The silence settled between them as they pondered what might lie in the future for them. They both jumped when it was broken by Harry, who had quietly observed everything from the sidelines.

"Don't suppose there's any chance of a cuppa ladies? This sea air has left me dry as chips."

Angela sprang to her feet. "I'm terribly sorry Mr Elliott. How rude of me. Both of you come into the kitchen while I put the kettle on. I have a million questions to ask yet, tea or coffee for starters?"

"Coffee for me thanks Angela, and hot chocolate for the little mother here if you have any." He chuckled, breaking the tension between the two women. "Oh, and for goodness sake, please call me Harry."

⁂

"Well that wasn't too bad," Harry confided, as they walked to his car. "Your mother took things pretty well I thought, all things considered."

"She's changed Harry. I hardly recognised her. Although she wouldn't admit it, I think she's not feeling too well, besides everything else." She paused as they got in. "Did you notice the half empty Vodka bottle in the kitchen? I think she's probably taking Aldo's leaving harder than mine, and living on her own doesn't suit her nature."

"Oh I don't know Cas. I think she seems okay. Maybe she'll pick up a bit when Cameron comes back home next week."

"I certainly hope so, but he doesn't sound too bright to me either." She laid a hand on Harry's arm and turned to smile at him. "Thanks Harry. You were right. I should have come sooner. Now, let's get this show on the road. I'm dying to get home and stretch out for an hour or so. This little critter doesn't seem to enjoy the sea air either," she added, rubbing her stomach. "It's been kicking me all day."

"Probably just excited at meeting Grandma for the first time," he chortled, and cringed as Cassie gave him a friendly slap on the shoulder.

CHAPTER FIFTEEN

As the due date for the arrival of Cassie's baby approached, she and Harry set about making provision for it. He had quietly suggested, or rather asked, if perhaps she should return to be with her mother, but Cassie wouldn't hear of it. Not only was she unsure if she could live with her again, but she had grown to value her independence. Besides, it wouldn't be fair to Harry who was looking forward to the birth as much as any real expectant father ever had. He would be devastated if she left now.

There was one other factor behind her decision. It was her blossoming friendship with Brad, who also seemed genuinely smitten with the imminent arrival of the baby. By now he was a regular visitor to their house, often insisting Cassie put her feet up while he prepared dinner for all three of them. He often sat chatting with her then long after Harry had gone to bed, as he lay listening to them whispering and giggling in the lounge room. I just hope he doesn't let her down like that mongrel Craig did, he thought.

Harry answered the knock on his door at one o'clock in the morning and found Cassie doubled over in pain in the hall.

"I'm sorry to wake you Harry," she muttered through gritted teeth. "I tried to wait till morning, but I don't think I can hold on that long."

He rushed to help her to her comfy chair. "Don't be silly Cas," he said. "I told you to call me whenever you needed me. Now, do you think you need to go to the hospital straight away?"

She nodded vigorously as she sucked in deep breaths as the anti-natal nurse had taught her. "I've put my suitcase at the door," she wheezed, and then, attempting a smile she added, "but you'd better put some clothes on first, don't you think?"

Suddenly realizing he was clad in nothing more than a pair of boxer shorts, he scurried back into his room. As he dressed he heard her talking on the phone. Ringing her mother maybe?

"That was Brad," she said in answer to the un-stated question on his face when he returned. "He made me promise to ring him when I went in. I think he wants to be there to help me. Do you mind?"

Actually, he did, just a little, but hid his disappointment. "No, of course not. Now come along. I'll get the car out."

❦

Ten hours later, Harry became the second man to see little Harriet Douglas when he visited the maternity hospital in his lunch hour. Exhausted but sublimely happy and proud, Cassie showed off her daughter to him.

"She's beautiful Cassie, just like her Mum," he said as he sat down beside her bed. "You must be very proud."

"I am Harry, and you should be too. She wouldn't be here if it wasn't for you. We both owe you so much," she said softly as she stroked the tiny hand protruding from the swaddling. "If she had been a boy I intended calling him Harry you know, but when I found out she was a girl I switched to Harriet. Don't you think it's a pretty name?"

"I do, and I am very honoured Casssie. I really am. It's more than I deserve. Thank you." Then, looking around, he added, "has Brad gone?"

"Yes. He had to go to work, but he stayed with me as long as he could. He was marvellous."

Again Harry felt a twinge of jealousy. I shouldn't be like this he thought to himself. He has been good to her, but memories of how Craig had treated her still stuck in his craw. He was determined to see she wasn't hurt again, at least while she was living in his house. He took a long look at Harriet's pink little face and was sure she was going to take after her mother. He certainly hoped so. He never wanted to hear or see the poor little thing's father again.

⅗

Unfortunately, that wish was not going to be fulfilled. While Harry had avoided any further contact with Craig through the Union or at work, his face stared back at Harry from the pages of a local paper a few weeks later. He had been selected as the Labor candidate in the forth-coming State election.

Just what you would expect of him Harry muttered to himself, flicking the paper shut. "What's that?" Cassie said as she came into the room.

Harry wondered for a second if he should tell her or not, but decided she was bound to find out in time anyway.

"It's that mongrel Craig," he rasped. "He's standing for parliament. There's no end to his ambition, or his cheek. Fancy someone like that wanting to represent us. The hide of the man. Just look at him," he said, turning up the article.

Cassie stared at the face she hadn't seen for months and realised she had mixed feelings. She hated him for what he had done, but he was the father of her beautiful little baby asleep in her bassinet, and always would be, no matter what happened in the rest of her life. True to the agreement they had reached, she had left his name off the birth registration certificate, and when

134

Harry had sent him a photo copy, Cassie had received a short note of congratulations and the promised five thousand dollar cheque. She assumed that was the last she would ever hear from him. How wrong she was.

"Forget him Harry," she said. "He's not worth worrying about. I have. Now, can I get you a cup of tea? I'm going to make a sandwich too. I'm starving."

"Let me help you little mother," he said, as they went through to the kitchen. Life has never been so good, he thought to himself, in spite of being woken up at all hours of the night. Only one thing spoilt their cosy little family relationship from his point of view, and he was ashamed to admit it to himself. He knew it was selfish of him, but he couldn't stop himself feeling resentment at the presence of Brad in their lives.

Hardly a day or night passed without a visit from him, and he noticed they had started greeting each other with a friendly kiss. Brad often drove her to the shops or took her and Harriet on little outings. Even an old bachelor like him could see that their friendship was turning into something much more. For the first time since she came to live with him, he was forced to share her with someone else, someone young and attractive. The writing was on the wall.

He shouldn't have been surprised then when it finally happened. After days of hesitation, Cassie finally agreed to let him baby-sit Harriet so Brad and she could go to a Bruce Springsteen concert. Armed with a list of instructions and a promise to ring during the interval, the young couple took off for what was Cassie's first proper date that he could recall. They looked like an excited pair of teenagers he thought, which of course, they almost were. When he heard them safely home well past midnight, he relaxed and went to sleep.

अॆ

The smell of frying bacon filled the kitchen as Harry set about preparing their traditional Sunday morning breakfast. He'd slept like a log, not even being woken by Harriet, and was looking forward to a day pottering in the garden. Cassie came in behind him, put her arms around him, and gave him a peck on the cheek.

"Thanks Harry," she said.

"You're welcome," he chuckled. "Have a good time?"

"Wonderful."

Harry noticed the apprehension in her voice and turned to look at her. She seemed worried.

"Everything okay Cas?" he asked, and then looked up as Brad came into the kitchen.

"Do you think we can stretch breakfast for three Harry?" she said, trying to sound more relaxed than she felt. "We seem to have picked up an extra boarder."

Harry hoped the shock he felt didn't show. "Hello Brad'" he managed. "I'm sure we can. Set another place Cas. I'll get some more bacon." With his head buried in the fridge, he missed the nervous glance that passed between them, the touch of hands as Brad came to her, and the blush on her face as he kissed her forehead.

Conversation over breakfast was strained and friendly enough, but restricted to the concert, Harriet, and Harry's garden. Eventually Brad thanked Harry for breakfast, said goodbye to them both and left.

Cassie found Harry hosing his roses. "I'm sorry Harry," she said simply. He didn't answer.

"It just happened last night. It was so late and I suggested Brad should stay and go home this morning. He was going to sleep on the lounge, but, well one thing led to another, and well, in the end, he slept with me," she blurted out.

Still Harry said nothing as he reached over and squashed an aphid on a bud.

"I think I love him Harry," she said quietly.

He turned to look at her. She was blushing, and looking most uncomfortable. This was obviously difficult for her and here he was making it worse. What kind of father figure was he? Turning off the hose and dropping it on the ground, he put his arm round her waist and led her to a garden seat.

"Come on Cas. Sit down here and tell me all about it," he said. Then to lighten the atmosphere a bit, he added, "well perhaps not ALL about it, just the parts you want to eh?" His friendly smile and salacious wink let her relax and she told him how much she had come to love Brad.

"And he loves me too Harry. I know he does, and he's marvellous with Harriet don't you think?"

"Of course I do love," he said. "You make a great couple. No, that's not right. You make a great threesome actually. Now, if you want to keep that going, you'd better go and give that girl her breakfast before she starves to death. I think I just heard her starting to whinge."

"Oh my God! Look at that time," Cassie gasped. "It's way past her feed time." Then, taking his hands in hers, she said, "Thanks for being so understanding Harry. You're a real gem." She planted a kiss on his cheek and hurried towards the door. Harry stayed on the seat for some time, staring into space and seeing nothing as he pondered on how much he had missed out on in his life.

CHAPTER SIXTEEN

Cassie was worried. In all the time she had been living with Harry she had insisted on paying rent and sharing the household costs. Not that she had to. He used to say to her what kind of de-facto father asks his daughter to pay board and lodgings, but she insisted, and he finally agreed. The deal she had struck with Craig gave her income till Harriet was born, and the cash payment had more than covered her medical expenses, but now, after three months without income, her savings were running low. She would have to find a job, and with a young baby to look after, that was not going to be easy.

Harry was keen to help, but he was a couple of years from retirement and still had to work his five day week. It was Brad who came up with the solution.

"So you see Harry, Brad can get me a part-time job as a cook's assistant in the kitchen where he works. He can organise it so I only work nights and weekends. I hate to ask, but would you mind looking after Harriet for me? I wouldn't trust anyone else."

"I don't suppose you would let me provide free board would you? Then you wouldn't have to work." She shook her head. "I thought so. Too independent for your own good, you are," he added. "Let me think about it eh? I'm not sure I would feel comfortable looking after a little baby on my own for more than a few hours. Maybe we can think of something else."

But they never did, and Cassie started work in the cafe with Brad, while Harry found himself changing nappies and bottle feeding his de-facto grand-daughter. He also found himself across the breakfast table with Brad more and more, as he was tending to stay the night more often. Like most parents, he wasn't entirely comfortable with this, but, again like them, he put up with it, hoping quietly to himself that their romance would blow over, and Brad would move on. The end came, but not how he had hoped. Brad left the scene, but he took Cassie and Harriet with him.

❦

"Aren't you happy for me Harry?" Cassie asked, disappointed at his obvious lack of excitement when she showed him her engagement ring.

Hiding more than lack of excitement, but actual bitter disappointment, he pulled her to him and said over her shoulder, "of course I am love. I wish nothing but the best for you."

"But?" she asked, detecting the doubt in his voice.

Harry forced a weak smile. "Just me being a selfish old man Cas. I can't imagine being on my own again. I'll miss you and little Harriet so much I can't tell you."

Now it was Cassie's turn to look uncomfortable. She and Brad had planned everything working on a different assumption. Perhaps they had taken too much for granted.

"That needn't happen, if you don't want it to Harry. Not for the time being anyway. Brad could move in here with us if it's okay with you. We could save up to buy a house with both of us working. We'd pay you board of course, and baby-sitting fees," she added with a broad smile. "And he'd cook and I'd wash up."

How could he refuse? He had come to love this girl as if she was his own daughter. Would any father say no to a request like that? Although he wasn't all that enamoured with Brad, he seemed to be a decent sort of bloke, who doted on Cassie, and accepted

Harriet in their lives. Besides, a full house would be preferable to the lonely one he was used to. Of course it wouldn't last forever, but maybe he should let the future look after itself. You never know what might turn up, he decided. So Brad moved in.

⚹

With Christmas approaching, Harry insisted that Cassie should bring Brad on their annual trip to Roma so Bill could meet not only his grand-daughter, but also his future son-in-law. Before that though, after much pestering, he also finally convinced her to take them both to see her mother. It just wasn't fair, he told her, to exclude her mother from such momentous events in her life. Also, if there was to be a wedding in the future, she should be part of it, although he wasn't sure how she and Bill could handle that. Time to worry about that another day, he decided. For now, he was happy enough to wave them off as they headed to the Coast. They were going to surprise her. If only he had known the disaster that was to follow, he would not have insisted.

Cassie had been taken aback at the sight of her mother on the previous visit, but now she was absolutely shocked at the appearance of the young man who opened the door to them at the unit. It was now more than four years since she had laid eyes on her brother, and she could scarcely accept that it was actually him. The good-looking young teenager she had last seen was no more. Before her stood, or rather slumped against the door frame, a skinny, long haired, bearded apparition with a sallow complexion, wearing nothing but a grubby looking pair of track pants.

"Yeah," he said, through eyes squinting at the sunlight. "Who are you, and what do you want?"

"My God!" Cassie gasped. "Cameron. You don't even know me."

141

He straightened up and peered at her more closely. "Cassie? Is that you?" His voice was raspy, and his hand trembled on the door knob.

Rattled as she was at his appearance, Cassie managed to mumble, "We've come to see Mum. Can we come in?"

He stiffened. "No," he blurted out. "I mean, I'm sorry, but she's not home." He drew the door a little more closed.

"We could wait," Cassie said hopefully. "We've come all this way. When will she be back?"

Cameron's eyes darted from Cassie to Brad to the baby and down to the floor. "She won't," he stammered, "or rather, she won't be back today. She's staying with a friend."

That would be right Cassie thought to herself. She's obviously found a replacement for Aldo. Good luck to her then. At least she could return to Harry with a clear conscience having tried, and without having a confrontation. As for Cameron, he didn't seem too pleased to see her and she didn't fancy a sisterly chat with him either. He probably had his own female company inside. Hitching Harriet up a notch higher on her hip, she glared back at him.

"Well obviously you don't want us to come in, so we'll be on our way then." He made no comment, avoiding her gaze. "Come on Brad," she said, turning away. "Let's go."

Before she had taken a step, she heard a call from inside the unit. Feeble though it was, and muffled by the almost closed door, she recognised it as her mother's.

"Who is it Craig?"

Panic swept his face. He drew back inside and tried to shut the door, but he was too late. Quick as a flash, Cassie's foot was wedged in the gap and she pushed past his feeble attempt to keep her out. The scene that met her gaze as she burst into the living room made her gasp. The room was a total mess, and there, sprawled on the sofa in the middle of it all, was Angela. Her emaciated frame was draped in a dirty looking robe. Dishevelled hair framed a haggard face with sunken eyes set in dark sockets. Her mouth fell open at the sight of her daughter. "Oh my God," she gasped as she struggled to clamber to her feet, but fell back against the cushions.

Cassie thrust Harriet into Brad's arms and rushed to help her. "Mum! What's the matter with you? Are you alright?"

Angela lay back with her eyes closed and teeth gritted. Cassie swung around to her brother. "For God's sake Cameron. Don't just stand there gawking. Get her a drink or something. Maybe you should call an ambulance." He didn't move.

"You'd better tell her Mum," he said.

"Tell me what, you moron? Can't you see she's sick?"

Angela laid a hand on her arm. "Don't yell at him Casandra," she almost whispered. She struggled into a sitting position. "It's not his fault." She paused and a sob escaped her throat. "There's nothing Cameron can do for me, or anyone else for that matter. I'm dying Casandra."

"NO!" Her scream hung in the air. Cameron walked away and disappeared into another room. Brad took Harriet into the kitchen as Cassie took her mother in her arms and held her close as silent sobs wracked her frail body. Tears ran down her cheeks as her mind tried to grapple with the situation.

A surge of emotions ran through her all at the same time. Pity for her mother who was obviously suffering and probably had been for some time. Memories of her drawn appearance on the last visit flooded back. She should have realised then something was not right. Remorse for her own actions in ignoring her mother for all those years. Perhaps it was the distress of her running away in the first place that brought on her illness. Disgust for Aldo who had deserted her in her hour of need to take up with someone younger and healthier. Disappointment because Cameron seemed to be completely useless, and finally, helplessness at her own inability to do anything about it.

She realised the sobbing had stopped, pulled a hankie from her pocket and handed it to Angela. Their eyes met. "Tell me Mum."

ત

The trip back to Brisbane seemed to take hours. Brad drove in silence and Harriet slept in her car seat, leaving Cassie trying to put in order the myriad of thoughts that swirled in her head.

Cameron must have snuck out through the back door as they never saw him again. And I never want to in the future, Cassie thought. He was obviously a complete junkie, and the thought of leaving her mother living with him left her distraught, but feeling helpless to do anything about it. All the animosity built up through their years of estrangement was washed away by the sight of the once glamorous Angela.

Obviously wracked by the cancer that had invaded her frail body, she struggled to manage the daily requirements of caring for herself, and probably her useless son too, Cassie thought with disgust. She should be moved to some form of care, but what could she do about that. Maybe Harry could suggest something. Or Brad.

She took a sideways glance at his grim face. "I'm sorry you had to see that Brad," she said, reaching across to lay her hand on his arm. "I had no idea what she was like, and now I have no idea what to do about it."

Brad said nothing, staring ahead as they ground their way up the M1. This was something he hadn't counted on when he proposed to Cassie. He loved her and thought they could build a great life together if given the chance. Of course Harriet was a bit of a complication. Most young blokes didn't start off their married life sharing it with some other man's baby.

Initially he had enjoyed the chance to help Cassie through her ordeal, but it wasn't all beer and skittles. At their stage of life, they should have been seeing the world before settling down to domesticity and family life. And now this turn-up. Surely Cassie didn't expect him to help that hopeless pair he had just met. He realised she was looking at him expectantly.

"I don't know what you can do Cas," he offered. "They're both adults you know, and you have enough on your plate already."

Cassie was taken aback at his obvious lack of sympathy. All of the bad blood that had developed between her and Angela over the years had disappeared instantly when she was faced with the pathetically frail figure of her mother sitting in a crumpled heap on the couch. She had kept her cancer problems to herself last time they met, but there was no hiding the obvious ravages now. She had only months to live, and Cassie felt all the love and respect of a daughter for a mother in such circumstances come flooding back to her.

Tears rolled down her cheeks. In spite of all that had happened between them in recent years, she couldn't desert her mother in her final days.

"I'm sorry Brad," she Mumbled. "I really am, but I just have to do something to help her. Maybe Harry will know what to do."

That would be right, Brad thought to himself. The marvellous Mr Elliott who she seemed to think could solve everything. Although he never let on, Brad was sure Harry resented the relationship that had developed between him and Cassie. They couldn't possibly continue to live in his shadow much longer. It was time to move on. He would look for a flat tomorrow.

CHAPTER SEVENTEEN

It was probably the hardest thing Cassie had ever had to do in her life, and that was saying something. Harder than her decision to run away from school. Tougher than having to deal with Craig, and even seeing her dying mother. She put it off for days until Brad insisted this was her last chance before he did it himself.

She had to break the news to Harry that they were moving out of his house, and she knew how disappointed he would be to lose her companionship, and that of Harriet too of course, but Brad had insisted, and finally she had given in to him. He had found a flat in the next suburb of Wilston, and they had to move in on the following weekend.

Harry's reaction was as pathetic as she had imagined it would be. While he did his best to hide his true feelings, in fact he was shattered. The last few years since Cassie moved in had been the happiest of his life. It made him realise just how much he had lost by not marrying and having a family of his own. It had almost happened once, but his mother had taken a selfish disliking to the girl he wanted to marry, and he had foolishly abided by her wishes and broken off their relationship. That was a big mistake. He had never found another woman to share his life with, and had been condemned to forty years of solitude.

Now, as he sat on a garden seat absent-mindedly pushing Harriett back and forth in her stroller while the young couple loaded up Brad's car with their meagre possessions, he reflected on how it had all started. What were the odds, he wondered, of him ever having met Cassie in the first place. He smiled sadly to himself as he recalled that he didn't even like Chinese food much, and had only been in that restaurant opposite the jewellers because his regular cafe had closed down.

What had induced him to even notice the young girl standing there, much less approach her when he thought she was in trouble? Ah, the quirks of fate that decided all that had followed over the last few years and had led to where he found himself today—losing the one person in his life he had come to love so much. Two actually, he decided, as he leaned forward to admire the sleeping form in the stroller.

He heaved a deep sigh. Still, all was not lost. They were only moving a few streets away, and he knew Cassie would visit as often as their busy life-style permitted. And then there was Harriet, he thought smiling smugly to himself. He may be losing his role as landlord to the parents, but he was pretty sure he would still be in big demand as a baby-sitter.

❧

Three weeks to the day after their trip to the Gold Coast, Cassie received a call that rocked her world again. Angela had died. The police officer who called her refused to give details of the circumstances, directing her instead to a solicitor who was the administrator of her mother's estate. After several minutes spent in trying to compose herself, she dialled the number that had been given to her.

"Good morning Miss Douglas," the voice had answered. "I'm Peter Bancroft, your mother's solicitor. Let me start by offering my sincere condolences. You must be extremely upset."

Of course she was upset. What a silly thing to say. "Thank you Mr Bancroft. I just can't believe my mother is dead. I know she was very ill, but I didn't think she was that close to death. What happened?"

There was a long pause on the line, followed by his hesitant reply.

"I'm afraid I can't really answer that yet Miss Douglas. The circumstances of her death are still being investigated I'm afraid. Apparently they are not quite certain as to exactly what has happened, but a neighbour rang triple zero yesterday because she could smell gas in the hallway. The police found Angela unresponsive on the kitchen floor. That's about all I can tell you at the moment."

"Oh my God," Cassie gasped. "Are you saying she committed suicide?"

"No. No I'm not saying that. Until the police finish their work and an autopsy is held, the cause of your mother's death will remain a mystery." He heard her sobbing on the line. "Are you alright?" He listened as she sucked in a deep breath and took control of herself before he continued.

"Under the terms of her will, I am the executor and administrator of her estate, and as such will be dealing with the authorities to finalise matters with them. I will then be in a position to meet with you and your brother to reveal the contents of the will. Is that all clear?"

He barely heard her whispered answer "Yes thanks," before the phone rang off.

Peter Bancroft was feeling really sorry for the young woman he had yet to meet, although he was very familiar with her circumstances. He had acted as Angela's solicitor since she used him to negotiate a divorce with that scumbag Aldo Mercini. He was also aware of her previous life on the farm and knew about the fractured relationship between mother and daughter. Now, just as they seemed to be getting back together, Angela was dead.

The terminal cancer sentence had really rocked her, and in his dealings with her he thought he had sometimes detected a suppressed wish to get her death over and done with, and now this. Cancer? Accident? Suicide? He wondered. Time would tell, he supposed.

ॐ

A week later Cassie was ushered into the plush tenth floor Surfers Paradise office of Peter Bancroft.

He greeted her at the door, shook her hand, and then gave her a brief hug as he once again mumbled his condolences before directing her to a comfortable chair.

"Thank you for coming Miss Douglas. Can I order you a coffee while we wait for your brother to arrive?"

It had been a long drive in the heavy traffic and she had left home on an empty stomach. "That would be lovely thanks Mr Bancroft, and please call me Cassie, or Cassandra as my mother always insisted on calling me." A smile flashed across his face as he left the room to speak to his secretary.

When he returned, he was accompanied by Cameron, causing Cassie to jump to her feet. She could scarcely believe her eyes. While he was still emaciated and somewhat sallow, he was clean shaven, sported a trim haircut, and was neatly dressed in slacks and casual shirt. His embarassed expression broke into a nervous grin as he offered his hand. "Hello Cas." She pulled him into a hug which gave the solicitor a chance to usher in his secretary with coffee and muffins.

Twenty minutes later, refreshed and keen to put an end to the strained small talk between the siblings, he gathered up his papers from the desk and sat to face them.

"This has obviously been a very difficult time for both of you," he began. "I'm sorry it has taken some time to reach the point where I could call you in to advise you of the outcome of all the various investigations into your mother's death. Please understand, this is just normal procedure in circumstances where there is any doubt as to a person's cause of death."

He noticed the accusatory glance that passed from Cassie to her brother, who stared impassively at the floor. There seemed to be no love lost between that pair he thought. He cleared his throat and continued.

"Apparently your mother died from inhalation of gas from the stove where one ring was found to be turned on, but not lit. Because of the debilitated state of her health, the police report concluded that she probably fell over after turning on the gas and was unable to regain her feet. There was also some indication of a possible heart attack too which reinforced their opinion that her death was accidental. There was no evidence of violence."

"Or suicide?" Cassie whispered.

"No. Not as far as they were concerned. She certainly didn't leave any message."

Cassie gazed at her brother for a few seconds and then asked the obvious question. "And where were you when this happened Cameron?"

"Away. I was with some friends at Nimbin."

"That figures. You left Mum to look after herself when she was so sick?"

Cameron shifted uneasily in his seat. "I didn't know she was that bad," he mumbled. "Besides, I didn't see you doing much to help her. That surprise visit with your boyfriend and baby didn't do much for her either. She cried for days after you left."

He enjoyed the look of shame that flashed across her face. He hadn't forgotten the disgust she had registered when he answered the door to her and Brad. It was alright for her to criticise him, but at least he was around most of the time. Now Angela's death had shocked him out of his drug fuelled stupor and he was determined to pull himself together. He turned to meet Cassie's fraught look.

"I'm sorry Cameron. I can't help feeling responsible in some part for her cancer. They say it can be caused by stress, and I certainly gave her plenty of that." She paused and then added, "we haven't been ideal kids have we?"

"Probably not," he conceded. "She had pretty high standards."

Peter Bancroft observed this reconciliation of sorts with some degree of relief. It might make what he had to tell them next a bit easier. He shuffled his papers and brought out the last will and testament which Angela had asked him to prepare only a few weeks ago. Rather than read out all the legalise in the document, he decided it might be more practical to give them a verbal summary.

"Let me start by assuring you both that your mother very much loved you both, in spite of all that has happened in your family. She also retained the highest respect for your father, and held no resentment towards him. As she put it to me, they just weren't well matched as things turned out. Her main regret was the impact that their divorce had on you two."

"We were okay until she hitched up with that slimy Aldo,"

Cassie said. "He turned her into the person she became. I just couldn't stand him."

Peter decided not to confide that Aldo Mercini was due to face court next week charged with conducting a Ponzi scheme that had cost most of his friends a fortune.

"Anyway," he continued, "to get down to the will itself, Angela has left the little value remaining in her estate to be shared equally between you. I'm afraid most of the money from her divorce settlements has been dissipated over recent times due to her illness. I know she was worried by her present circumstances."

That knowledge had led him to jump to the immediate conclusion of suicide when he heard the circumstances of her death. Maybe he was right, but the police had been unable to prove that to be the case, and he had never indicated his suspicions to them, or anyone else for that matter. Much better for all concerned if her death was accepted to be a tragic accident, but looking at the thoughtful expression on Cassie's face, he wondered if perhaps the thought had crossed her mind too. He hurried on.

"By the time all of her legal and funeral expenses are taken care of, each of you will probably receive a few thousand dollars. As executor, I will attend to all the details and keep you informed of developments. You had better leave me forwarding addresses before you go," he added, pointedly looking at Cameron. He had a sneaking suspicion his future probably lay in some share house at Nimbin, in spite of his improved appearance. Once caught by the drug menace it was almost impossible for a young person to escape, especially one who lacked any form of family support.

Perhaps Cassie might be prepared to help him, he wondered. He had observed that people often turned towards each other in times of adversity, or indeed, bereavement. Maybe he could help. "Listen," he said as he stood. "Why don't I get my secretary to book a table for you at the restaurant across the road where you can have a nice lunch on me. I'd come with you if I could, but unfortunately I'm rather busy today. Besides," he added with a smile, "you two will probably want to put these sad circumstances behind you for a while and talk of better times eh?"

I wish, he thought to himself as he guided them through the front office, but you never know, and they probably had a happy childhood on the farm before Angela tore their little family apart by leaving. Anyway, a bloke can only try, he thought wryly.

❧

So many thoughts were running through Cassie's mind as she returned to Brisbane that she had trouble concentrating on her driving and stuck resolutely to the slow lane all the way.

For the moment she put her mother's death aside while she tried to deal with a new complexity in her life...Cameron. Other than the brief confrontation with him a few weeks before, she had not spoken to him for years. He was probably just as shocked with her sudden appearance as she had been with his.

After a very shaky start, their lunch together had given them an opportunity to mend a few bridges, and to bring each other up to date on their lives since Cassie ran away. The drug habit he picked up in Thailand had drained his health and self esteem, and probably Angela's bank account too, but her death seemed to have brought him to his senses. He was determined to turn over a new leaf, and determined to stay clean, get a job and find somewhere to live.

After the pre-paid rent on the unit ran out in a few days he would be homeless, and Cassie had fleetingly thought of offering to take him in, or even asking Harry to put him up for a while, but had decided the risk was too great. Better to let him find his own feet like she had. Maybe she could suggest to the solicitor that he lend him an advance from his inheritance. She would ring when she got home to thank him for the lunch and make the suggestion about Cameron. Other than the fifty dollar note she slipped to him. It was the least she could do for the brother she had once looked up to so much. How they had both changed since their days on the farm.

CHAPTER EIGHTEEN

Harry was a worried man. Although he couldn't quite put his finger on what it was that was worrying him, his concerns had grown every time he'd seen Cassie lately. She still visited him several times each week, including when he minded little Harriet for her. Her bubbly personality had disappeared, replaced by something much more reserved and serious. Of course it could just be her growing maturity, pressure from work, or even the normal strains of rearing a baby, but in the pit of his stomach, he felt there was something else.

On several occasions he had almost broached the subject, but in the end, felt that perhaps it was none of his business. After all, he wasn't her father, no matter how much he wished he could have been, and little Harriet's grand-father he thought with a smile. What a terrific little thing she was and how he enjoyed his time alone with her. A frown crossed his brow as he suddenly realised she had also changed lately. Seemed more jumpy somehow, less settled, and often woke crying from a sound sleep.

These thoughts were on his mind as he opened the door for his two favourite people one Sunday morning, and then he noticed the bruises. Both were on Cassie's upper arms. As he put the kettle on he made the decision to voice his concerns. Nodding at her arm he asked, "Run into a door Cas?"

"Oh that," she replied, following his indication. For a moment she looked uncomfortable, then forced a smile. "Yes, actually that is what happened when I went to check on Harriet in the dark. Clumsy aren't I?"

When she met his level gaze, she blushed and looked away.

"More than clumsy I'd say love, when you must have done the same the next night too by the look of your other arm."

Cassie crossed her arms, covering both bruises with her hands, and turned away from him. Harry put his arm around her shoulders, and could feel the sobs she was trying so hard to suppress. He gently led her to the couch and held her as put her face in her hands and cried silently. The kettle whistled on the stove and Harry left her to compose herself while he made a pot of tea. As he laid the tray on the coffee table he was pleased to see that the determined look he was so used to had returned. "Here Cas," he said. "You be mother." It even brought forth a wan smile.

She poured the tea in silence, while Harry waited patiently for her to open the conversation that they both knew what was long overdue.

"I'm sorry Harry," she began. "I really am. I should never have lied to you, of all people. You saved my life and have been so good to us. I'm just so sorry."

"You don't have to say sorry to me Cas. I should be apologising to you for being an old nosey parker and upsetting you in the first place. You needn't tell me about it if you don't want to. It's really none of my business."

She sipped her tea in silence for a few moments, replaced her cup, drew in a deep breath, and opened up.

"Brad did it. He didn't mean to, but he was so angry that he grabbed me by the arms and shook me. He didn't hit me or anything, I bruise easily I'm afraid. I should have worn long sleeves."

Harry said nothing.

"It was my fault. I'd made him mad by saying I wished I'd

never left here. You know how it is Harry. In the heat of the moment you say things that you don't really mean. Trouble is, recently it's been true."

Harry said nothing.

"He's changed since we moved into the flat. He's nothing like he was when we were living here. I feel like a complete stranger to him at times. Worse than that even, I think he now resents Harriet, after being so nice to her earlier."

Harry said nothing but took a sidewise glance at his namesake sleeping soundly in her stroller.

"I'm sorry Harry. I shouldn't be worrying you with all this rubbish," she said with a strained smile. "I'll get over it I suppose."

By the time they left him alone again Harry had managed to get a fair indication of how things really were between Cassie and Brad, and he was more worried than ever now he knew it wasn't just his imagination that had been bothering him. That young man had never impressed him, and he found it easy to accept what Cassie told him to be factual, but a new concern now caused him to shudder as Harriet waved him goodbye. What if he started mistreating her? What if he already was? Without openly suggesting as much to Cassie, he hoped he had at least put her on guard to the possibility. If only little Harriet was old enough to talk.

Nothing more to do, he decided, but to wait and see how it turned out, but he was getting nervous.

❧

That was probably why he nearly jumped out of his skin when there was a loud banging on the door a few days later, just as he was settling down to watch the news on telly. He was confronted by a distraught Cassie clutching Harriet in her arms. She hurried inside as he checked the street only to see the retreating light of a taxi in the distance. It seemed like his worse expectations had come to pass. He found Cassie rocking an upset baby in the kitchen. He could not fail to notice the red weal on her cheek.

"The bastard's done it Cassie, hasn't he? He's gone too far this time," he said. "I'm not letting you go back there with him. Come and sit down and tell me about it."

There were no tears this time, just a stoic look of determination that reminded him once again of the resolute little girl he had befriended years before.

"It was shocking Harry," she gasped. "He actually hit me. I couldn't believe it."

"What was it this time Cassie? Not me again I hope?"

"Well not directly, but it was your concern for Harriet's safety that set me thinking, and worrying. You were right. She has been much less settled recently. She used to be such a good little thing, hardly ever crying, but lately she starts crying for no reason at all, especially when she's with Brad. Sometimes she looks at him when he picks her up and bursts into tears."

They both looked at her as she lay between them on the sofa, eyes swinging from one to the other. Cassie went on.

"Today I was talking to the lady in the flat next door. She's a nice old thing who normally keeps to herself, but when I mentioned that Harriet seemed to be crying a lot recently a funny look crossed her face. What do you think it might be I asked her? She paused for a moment and then said that perhaps I should ask that young man I lived with. What are you saying I asked? Well it's not my business she replied, but when you're at work and he's looking after your baby she cries nearly all the time.

I couldn't believe what I was hearing Harry, but she obviously wasn't making it up. There had to be more to it, so I went in and confronted him. The truth came out. You wouldn't believe the things he said about her. He resents everything about her, while telling me all the time how dear she is to him. I called him a lying pig and he hit me. Then he stormed off. I assume he's gone to work.

Harry, I need your help again. Please. No, WE need your help. We've got to get away."

Two hours later, they had retrieved all of their possessions from the flat, loaded them into Harry's car, and booked into a nearby motel. Cassie was obviously scared stiff of Brad's reaction when he returned from work and found them gone. The first place he would look for them would be at Harry's house, and neither of them wanted to be there if he came knocking on the door in the middle of the night. While Cassie packed, Harry had rung her father who had insisted they should come and stay with him, at least until Brad had disappeared from the scene. Early next morning they headed west.

It had been a busy morning for Bill Douglas as he worked valiantly to make his bachelor pad more presentable for his visitors. More than visitors, he thought to himself as he vacuumed the lounge room floor. They were family, even Harry. What a great bloke he was. They all owed him so much.

He jumped as he heard a car pull up at the front of the house, and he rushed to open the door, but it was his parents, laden with the groceries and provisions he had asked them to bring out for him, including a pack of disposable nappies. Ever the practical farmer, he thought.

He had no idea how long they intended to stay. Harry had been brief in his phone call from the flat, merely indicating that Cassie wanted to stay with him for a while. He suspected a broken relationship, but, assuming Cassie might be listening, he didn't ask any questions. From a selfish point of view he hoped it might last a while. He had a lot of catching up to do with his daughter, and grand-daughter, and his mother was just as excited as him. Another car pulled up, and a new chapter in his life began.

CHAPTER NINETEEN

"Grandad! Grandad! Look what we found." An excited little Harriett charged into the lounge where Bill was reading the *Country Life* and showed him a bucket containing half a dozen hen eggs. He sat her up on his knee and gave her a hug.

"So where did you find them Muppet?" he asked, giving her a tickle in the ribs.

She squirmed and giggled and then with big blue eyes wide open said "under the old trailer near the shed. I saw her come out cackling this morning so I told Mum where to look."

"Well that's just great. We'll have some of them for breakfast tomorrow eh? How about you put them in the kitchen? Where is your mum?"

"Right here," Cassie said as she came and flopped down beside him. "Isn't she a clever little girl grandad? She follows those chooks around like a sheep dog, and has even given them all names."

Bill chuckled, as he patted Harriet gently on the head. "Well she might have been a city slicker when she came here but it looks like we might make a farmer out of her yet eh?"

❧

Time had passed quickly for Bill since his little family had arrived on his doorstep two years ago with all their possessions packed in the boot of his friend Harry's car. He had been appalled at what they told him about Brad, and thankful that Cassie had the sense and courage to leave him when she saw what he was like. Too many women made excuses for the actions of their violent

162

partners and sometimes paid for it with their life, or that of their baby.

Given her experiences, firstly with Craig and then Brad, it was no surprise that she seemed to be steering clear of men since her return to the farm. Bill had expected her to return to the city once she was satisfied it was safe to do so, but to his surprise, and delight, she showed no inclination to leave. Quite the opposite in fact.

After a few weeks of settling in and bringing the old farm house up to her meticulous standard, she arrived home with the shopping one day to tell him she had been offered a job at the local IGA, provided of course the two older generations were prepared to help with baby sitting. She need not have asked. The three of them took to the task with gusto, and they were now a close knit four generation family.

The only concern Cassie had with her decision to stay was the sense of guilt she felt towards her friend and mentor Harry. After all he had done for her, he was now back living his lonely life in Brisbane. His retirement had made things worse, with so much time on his hands, and no-one to share it with. She even asked if he would like to come and live on the farm. He considered for a while, but felt he would be intruding, and besides, he had always been a city slicker, so he settled back into his old life, with only Soxy for company. His annual visits to the farm over Christmas became the highlight of his year. And then they stopped.

"How's Harry going Dad?" Cassie asked as Bill came out of his office and flopped into his favourite chair. When he didn't answer, she glanced at him and saw a look of utter despair on his face. She put her arm around him. "What is it Dad? What's wrong?"

"He's not coming for Christmas Cas. He's not well enough."

"That's terrible news Dad. Harriet will be so disappointed. Maybe he can come later when he's better."

Bill sighed deeply and turned to her. "I don't think so love. The thing is, he's not going to get better." He paused to let realisation set in and heard her gasp.

"You don't mean...."

"Yes. I'm afraid so. Harry has stage four prostate cancer. It's reached the point of being untreatable I'm afraid. Poor old Harry won't be around much longer."

"NO!" she cried. "It can't be true. Not Harry."

Bill sat quietly and waited as the reality of the situation sank in and she accepted the devastating news he had delivered to her. Eventually she whispered to him.

"He saved my life Dad. I've never told you how our lives crossed in the first place, and I don't think I ever will, but believe me, without Harry I would have ended up in real trouble. I owe him so much, and now this."

"From what he told me Cas, there's nothing anyone can do for him now, but I'm sure he knows how much you love him. He asked me to help you accept the inevitability of the situation and to get on with your own life."

She turned to look at him. "Will you do that Dad please? The first thing I must do is go to see him. Will you look after Harriet for a couple of days?"

"Of course I will love. Don't you worry about us. When will you go?"

"As soon as I can line up time off work. Probably tomorrow," she said as she hopped up and headed for her phone.

✣

Cassie had been devastated by the news. Now as she glided down the Toowoomba range road tears welled to her eyes as her mind went back to the fateful day when she had run away from school down this same road. What a crazy thing to do. She could have landed in real trouble, but for the timely intervention of two people. Mrs Jones had taken her in when she was desperate, and Harry Elliott had saved her from her own foolish actions. And now, her very best friend in the world was dying.

The over-night stay proved to be rather traumatic for both of them. It was hard to accept the fact that this could well be their last meeting. Harry had quickly ruled out the idea of Cassie coming back to look after him. She had her own life to live now. Besides, he had put his house on the market and had booked himself into a near-by retirement home where he would be well looked after for the rest of his life.

Next morning, after a tear filled farewell, Cassie headed home, this time with a passenger in the car. Resplendent in his new cage sat Soxy, off to a new life in the place of his birth.

✣

He yawned and stretched as Cassie lifted him out of the car and carried him up the steps. She could hear voices and footsteps rushing to meet her. The door burst open.

"Mummy. Mummy," shouted an excited Harriet. "You're back. Look who's here" she said, pointing to a shy looking little boy hanging back in the hallway.

"Who have we here darling?"

"His name's Timmy. He's my new friend, aren't you Timmy?

Look what my Mummy brought. It's a cat. Can I play with it? What's its name?"

"Here, steady on a bit chatterbox," Bill said as he joined them. He picked up the little boy and brought him to where Cassie was cuddling her excitable daughter.

"Welcome back love," he said. "As you already know, this is Timmy. Timmy Parker to be precise. I'm minding him for his Dad while he's in town. I'll tell you about it later," he added as he saw the perplexed look on his daughter. "Now you'd better let that cat go so this pair can play with it while you and I catch up over a cuppa and some of the scones Grandma made for us yesterday."

※

"So that's it Cas. Another sad story I'm afraid. Tragic really, and Glen's such a nice young bloke. He didn't deserve this."

Bill had explained that Timmy belonged to the son of a long time mate who owned a property about fifty kilometres further west. The property had been in the family for generations, and when the only son Glen had married a local girl and produced a son, the future looked to be assured. Then disaster struck the young family. Travelling home from town at dusk one day about a year ago, his wife struck a roo, rolled the car and was killed. Poor little Timmy was just two years old.

"Probably explains why he's so shy and quiet I suppose," Bill said. "I feel sorry for young Glen, but he seems to be handling things okay lately. When I heard he needed to come this way on his way to town I suggested he should drop Timmy off to play with Harriet for a few hours. I'm sure she's nearly driven him nuts with her constant chatter. Just look at her will you?" he said, nodding towards the window.

Heading across the yard, bucket in one hand and Timmy in the other, Harriet was off on one of her chook watching and egg hunting expeditions. It brought a smile to the faces of the watching father and daughter.

❧

Cassie was busy peeling onions for a stir fry when she heard the Toyota pull up in front of the house. Bill met the occupant at the front door, along with a still chattering Harriet and a very relieved Timmy. With eyes watering, she turned as they came into the kitchen, and her heart missed a beat.

"This is Glen Cas, come to reclaim his son if he can prize him away from that daughter of yours."

Her gaze fell on a lanky good looking bloke, dressed in RM Williams gear, and nervously tossing his Akubra from hand to hand. With a shy grin, he moved forward, right hand outstretched. "G'day Cas," he said.

Cassie wiped her hands on her apron and shook it. "I'm sorry," she said through bleary eyes. "Onions and I don't agree I'm afraid. Give me a minute to wash my face will you? I'll be right back."

When she returned, the two men were enjoying a beer in the lounge. Noticing her glance at the stubbies, Bill said, "just the one Cas, then Glen's off home with that noisy son of his."

"Why don't you talk them into staying for tea Dad?" she said, once again running her eyes over their visitor. "I'll get back to my onions and throw an extra one in if you like."

"Good idea Cas. I reckon a big young bloke like this could handle a second stubbie and still be under the limit," he said winking at Glen. "Besides, he'd be unlucky to get put on a bag between here and Somerset Park," he added with a chuckle.

❧

The wedding of Cassie Douglas and Glen Parker took place six months later. From that very first night, they hit it off, both families were delighted that their somewhat shattered lives had been put back together. Their blended family settled in at Somerset Park.

Cassie thought that all the traumas of her time in the city were behind her, and that she would never cross paths again with boyfriend Brad, or Harriet's father Craig Thomas. How wrong she was. By a quirk of fate, their paths would cross again, but this time with vastly different consequences.

CHAPTER TWENTY

"Come on you two. Get in the car," Cassie yelled out as she strapped baby Cory into his car seat. "And don't forget your bags."

She smiled to herself as "Hurricane Harriet" charged through the fly screen door and ran to the car. She was already in and belted up in the front passenger seat when "Tardy Tim" carefully let himself out, closed the door and calmly took his place in the back seat.

"When's it going to be my turn in front Mum?" he asked.

"I guess when you beat your sister to the car Timmy. You'll have to start early to do that though. Now, have we thought of everything this morning? Haven't forgotten your homework?"

"Oh oh. Sorry," Timmy said as he slipped out of the car and headed back inside.

Cassie couldn't hide a smile at the raised eyebrows and look of exasperation on her daughter's face.

They were such great kids, but so totally different, she thought as she drove them to the little two teacher school down the road. In spite of this, they had become totally committed to each other. She was reminded of the relationship she and Cameron had enjoyed at the same age, with he being the dominant one leaving her trailing along behind. Hopefully, this pair wouldn't end up like her and Cameron whom she hadn't seen or heard from since Angela's funeral.

She dropped them off at the school gate and was about to drive off when she heard a call from the school.

"Yoo-hoo! Cassie. Could I see you for a minute please?"
It was the senior teacher who came hurrying out to the car. "Don't get out," she said. "There's just something I need to tell you. Bad news I'm afraid."

Cassie opened the passenger door for her to slip into the seat. "What's happened Judy? Has Harriett been talking in class again? Don't tell me you're going to expel her?"

The teacher smiled. "No nothing like that. She's my little helper in class, almost like a teacher's aid sometimes." She became serious again. "No. It's much worse than that I'm afraid. I've had a letter from the department. Cassie, they're going to close the school at the end of the year."

"They can't," Cassie gasped. "What are we expected to do? Home-school?"

"Either that, or catch buses into town with up to an hour each way for the out-lying kids. It's crazy. And just when we were achieving such success too, but apparently our student numbers don't measure up to the new Minister's guidelines."

"That's terrible. We can't stand for this Judy. I'm going to organise the parents to fight this. Can you show me the letter?"

"Sure. I'll get it." She returned and thrust it through the window. Cassie read it in disbelief, but it was the signature at the bottom that left her speechless.

The Honourable Craig Thomas....Minister for Education.

The colour drained from her face, and the letter dropped to her lap.

"My God Cassie," Judy gasped. "Are you alright? What's wrong?"

"Sorry. It's just that I know him. The Minister that is."

"Well that's wonderful. Do you think you might be able to get him to change his mind?"

Cassie sat staring at the signature that was so familiar to her. So that's where he's ended up, she thought. She knew it was always his intention to ride the union into parliament, but since moving back to Roma she had forgotten all about him. Now, here he was again messing up her life.

She turned back to the teacher. "Sorry Judy. I was just thinking of something that happened to me a long ago. In answer to your question, probably not, but know what, I'm going to try. Do you think you could find out which other remote schools have received similar notice and give me a list of them? I'd like to see if I can convince The Honourable Minister to change his mind.

A germ of an idea had sprung to her mind, and when Judy advised her of at least ten other small country schools that were on his hit list, she decided to act. Convinced that appealing to Craig's better nature wouldn't work, she embarked on another plan to save not only her school, but the others as well.

Cassie had never told Glen how Harriet had been conceived, merely saying it was a relationship that didn't last. It was now time to give him the details and elicit his support for what she intended to do. If her plan back-fired, her family could be involved, so he had to know. On the other hand, if things went according to plan, she could achieve her aim and only she would ever know how why. It all came down to her judgement of Craig's ego and personal ambition.

First up, she wrote to the Minister seeking a meeting to discuss the closure of her school, signing it Mrs G. Parker. A smug reply arrived indicating the decision had already been made, but if Mrs Parker still wished to see him, he would give her a few minutes of his time. How very nice of him she thought, and could hardly wait to see the look on his face when Mrs Parker was ushered into his office.

Now, armed with a list of the threatened schools, two letters, and a small plastic bag and its contents, she headed to Brisbane.

❧

"There's a Mrs Parker to see you Mr Minister," the pretty young assistant in the front office said on the phone.

Cassie wondered if she and Craig had anything going on between them. She had found out that he was still married, but that hadn't worried him before. For the young woman's sake, she hoped not, as she followed through the door with the Ministerial plaque. She was not disappointed at his reaction. He sprang to his feet.

"Cassie," he gasped. "It's you!"

"Hello again Craig. Nice to see you again," she purred as she held out her hand.

Craig was obviously rattled and struggling to regain composure as he ushered her to a seat.

"So Cassie," he said. "Mrs Parker now eh? Congratulations. Who's the lucky man?"

"Quite obviously, Mr Parker. We've been married for three years now. How is Mrs Thomas?"

Cassie enjoyed the mild panic that crossed his face.

"She's well," he managed.

"And your children?"

"Yes, growing up, of course."

She was enjoying this.

"Mine too. All three of them, including Harriet of course."

The verbal jousting had given Craig time to compose himself, and after eying her coolly for a few seconds, he asked in a flat voice, "Why are you here Cassie, or should I call you Mrs Parker?"

"No Cassie is fine thanks Craig. After all, we do know each other rather well don't we?"

He didn't answer, but waited on her answer.

"I'm surprised you don't know Mr Minister," she replied. "I'm here representing the small schools in remote areas of the State that have been issued closure notices. I hope to be able to get you to reconsider your decision."

Watching him carefully for his reaction, she could almost feel the usual air of confidence she remembered so well return to him. The conversation was now back in his field, and he relaxed visibly in his ministerial chair. He picked up the phone. "Joey, would you bring us in some coffees please? White with one for Mrs. Parker."

"You remembered Craig. I'm flattered."

"I've never forgotten you Cassie, and I'm sorry things didn't work out too well between us in the past, but as you can see, things have moved on, for both of us. You obviously have a new life, and so have I. Now here we are to discuss this little problem of school closures. I wish it was a simple matter and I could help you, but I'm afraid my hands are tied."

The conversation stopped as Joey brought the coffee. Cassie watched as Craig gave his a stir, licked the spoon, and placed it on his saucer, a habit of his that Cassie had never forgotten.

They debated the closure for twenty minutes, but Cassie could see she was making no headway. His mind was made up, and all of her good arguments fell on deaf ears. Finally he stood and offered his hand. "I'm sorry I haven't been able to help you Cassie. These decisions are tough, but necessary I'm afraid. If there's anything I can do about bus runs for example, let me know won't you?"

As he turned to escort her to the door, he didn't notice her take his teaspoon and slip it into her purse. Time for Plan B.

❧

Two weeks later, a very cool and composed Cassie walked straight into the front office of the Minister for Education.

"Good morning Joey," she said with a smile. "Remember me? Mrs Parker."

To say Joey looked flustered would be an understatement.

"Mrs Parker!" she gasped. "Do you have an appointment?"

"No I'm afraid I don't, but I wondered if you could squeeze me in for just a minute or two. I have something I would like to return to the Minister personally."

"Well it is rather against our rules and procedures I'm afraid. The Minister never sees anyone without an appointment."

Cassie smiled sweetly at her. "Would you mind asking him please?"

As Joey picked up the phone, Cassie stepped back and failed to pick up the short whispered conversation she had with her boss. The response was not what she expected.

"I'm sorry Mrs Parker. The Minister is very busy preparing some legislation. Perhaps you could make an appointment for another day?"

Cassie was irate. I'll bet he is, she thought. Probably thinking up some other union backed idea to kick country people in the guts. Well stuff him. I came all the way back here to have this out with him and I'm not leaving until I do. Ignoring his uncomfortable looking secretary, she charged across the room, flung open the door, and slamming it behind her, stood fair-square in front of a gaping Craig Thomas.

Joey rushed in too, obviously panicking. "I'm sorry Minister," she spluttered. "I told her you couldn't see her, but she just ignored me."

Craig waved her back to her office. "It's okay Joey. Mrs Parker sometimes doesn't take no for an answer. It's not your fault. I'll give her a couple of minutes now she's here." The door closed quietly behind her.

Craig leaned back in his big leather chair.

"That was a bit rude of you Cassie," he said."I would have thought your past experience as my personal assistant would have taught you better."

Cassie glared back at him. "My experience as your personal assistant, as you put it, taught me a lot of things Craig, including what a bastard you can be where your own self preservation is concerned. I also learned a thing or two about how to handle someone like you. My last visit showed it's a waste of time appealing to your better nature, so this time, I'm here to appeal to the other side of your nature...self preservation."

By now, she could see she had him worried. A frown crossed his brow as he leaned forward in his chair and started to reach for the phone.

"I wouldn't do that Craig, at least not till you hear me out."

He pulled his hand back, and sat back in his chair.

"Okay. You've got two minutes, but I warn you, if it's about school closures, you're wasting your time. The decision has been made and announced, and there's nothing I can do about it. Even if I wanted to," he added meaningfully.

"What a shame Craig, or should I say Mr Minister. Perhaps you may have to reconsider after all when I show you these two papers," Cassie said sweetly, as she withdrew two sheets from her handbag, handing him the top one. "As you can see, this is a formal agreement between you, as Minister for Education, and the group of remote country small schools I represent. You will note it commits you to recall all the closure letters, and to commit to keeping all ten of them open for so long as you are the responsible Minister. Simple as that. I'm sure you will be able to find a way to justify an about face. Blame the Department, or community pressure. Whatever you like, but that's the bottom line."

She watched as his expression changed from surprise, to anger and finally contempt.

"You must be mad. There is no way I would go back on that decision, especially now after you've burst in here uninvited and virtually threatened me. I think it's time for you to Leave Cassie." He again reached for the phone.

"Not yet Craig," she said in a low menacing voice that caused his hand pause in midair. "You haven't considered my other letter yet. It just might change your mind." She handed him the second sheet of paper and watched the colour drain from his face as he realised the contents. He threw it back to her.

"What's this rubbish all about?" he snarled.

"This rubbish, as you so elegantly put it Craig, is a certificate indicating that DNA tests have proven that you are Harriet's father, beyond all doubt. Of course, this isn't news to you, but other

176

than poor old Harry who is now dead by the way, no-one else knows you committed adultery with your secretary in your pre-parliamentary career as a Union official. Not the press, not your current secretary, not your Premier, and certainly not your good wife. All that could change."

"This is blackmail," he snapped.

"Call it what you like Craig. I call it repaying an old debt. Besides, I haven't linked it to the other letter asking you to change a departmental decision. What I intend to do with this one," she said, as she folded it and returned it to her handbag, "might or might not be influenced by your decision with respect to the school closures. I will decide what to do with it in one month's time. I might decide to burn it and never mention its findings to anyone. On the other hand...." She left the words hang in the air.

He stared at her in disbelief. This could be the end of the Parliamentary career he had worked so hard for. His straight-laced Premier would never support him through a scandal like this, and as for his marriage such as it was, well it would be over too. If Cassie made this public he was finished, particularly now she could prove it. Or could she, he wondered.

"I don't believe that report is genuine. How did you ever get a DNA sample from me anyway?"

Cassie gave him one last stare, then said "that's for me to know and you to wonder about Craig, but believe me, it's genuine. Certified by one of your own departments in fact." With that, she let herself out of his office, closing the door behind her.

As she passed Joey's desk she pulled a teaspoon from her bag and handed it to her. "Please give this to Craig for me Joey. Tell him I borrowed it last time I was here."

CHAPTER TWENTY ONE

As daylight crept through the house, Cassie crept from room to room kissing her sleeping children gently on the forehead. Cody didn't even stir and Timmy mumbled "Bye Mum" in his sleep, but as she went into Harriet's room, the bed-light came on, and showed a fully awake daughter sitting up in bed.

"It's too early for you to be awake pet. Are you all right?" she asked feeling her forehead for a temperature.

"I'm not sick Mummy, just excited. I've been waiting for sports day to arrive for weeks now, and today's the day."

A wave of guilt swelled in Cassie's mind as she looked at her excited little daughter. Her mind went back to the day a similar sport's day had split her family asunder when she was about the same age as Harriet. Of course things were different then. Her parents were drifting apart and the events of that traumatic day merely the catalyst for the inevitable separation that followed. Her guilty feelings only worsened when, as she leaned forward for a hug, Harriet whispered, "I wish you could come too Mummy."

She held her close for a moment as tears welled to her eyes.

"Yes, I know darling. I'm terribly sorry, but Mummy's just got to go to this meeting about your school. We don't want it to close do we, and Daddy will be there with you."

The audible sigh nearly broke her heart. "I know Mummy. Maybe next time eh? I'm going to win anyway, but I don't think Timmy will. He's too slow."

"Don't be so rude," Cassie laughed. "You look after him for me won't you?"

She gave a final hug and turned to leave. "Good luck baby."

ֆ

When she reached the highway she turned right and headed for Charleville where she was due to meet with parents from the ten small schools who had all received letters reversing the previous closure notices. Their letters had stated that the decision had been taken "following a further review of the situation by the department." No mention was made of the one person delegation which had led to the decision, but all of the parents and teachers involved knew that Cassie had somehow been able to work a miracle on their behalf and thought she must have been very persuasive.

Hardly persuasive she thought. People like Craig could not be persuaded to do anything against their will. But he could be black-mailed, Cassie thought with a wry grin. All it took was a lucky break to obtain a DNA sample from him, plus a few of Harriett's hairs brought from home, and he was left with no option but to capitulate.

No letter or phone call to her. Nothing. Just a change of decision, hiding behind the poor people in his department. How could he have known for sure she wasn't bluffing? That spoon must have convinced him. Fortunately, she now had that proof of parenthood safely in her keeping and she was confident Minister Craig Thomas would not cause any more trouble for her little group of schools who were now gathering to honour her efforts.

Looking at her watch as she drove into Mitchell, she decided there was time for a quick coffee and bite to eat. Thanks to her marvellous husband, she thought. Glen was such a stickler for leaving early and arriving on time. As she waited for her toasted muffins to arrive, her thoughts returned to her little family back on the farm. How lucky she had been to find him. Their blended family had worked from day one, and now, with little Cody joining them, her world was complete. Nothing was more important to her than family, all four generations of it.

As the muffins arrived, it suddenly hit her. What was that thought she just had? Nothing was more important to her than family. And here she was putting a celebratory lunch singing her praises ahead of her own daughter's big day. Regret, remorse, and finally panic caused her to feel sick in the stomach. Here she was doing exactly what Angela had done to her, and for similar reasons. Had she learnt nothing from the events that almost ruined her life? What had she been thinking?

Throwing some cash on the table beside her untouched muffins, she hurried back to her car, did a U-turn, and hurried back east.

❧

"Contestants for the under ten girls hundred metres please go to the starting line," the P.A. system blared.

"Away you go Harry," Glen said, giving her a pat on the back. "Good luck."

As the runners milled about at the start, their attention was drawn to a woman running flat out from the parking lot, calling out as she pushed through the crowd of parents.

"Harriet! Harriet! It's me. I'm here."

The two met in a huge hug, as the crowd stood watching perplexed and the starter began to line up the runners in their lanes.

"Off you go baby," Cassie said. "Go and do your best. I'll be cheering for you."

Harriet had a smile from ear to ear. "I knew you'd come Mummy. Now I know I'll win."

When the starter's gun fired, Cassie hardly heard it, as she and Glen clung together.

"What on earth happened to your day?" Glen asked.

"Reality struck dear," she replied. "I suddenly realised that nothing should come in the way of you and the kids. Nothing, and from now on, nothing will. I promise."

A red faced Harriet ran up. "Mummy! Mummy! I won. I told you I would."

"So did I darling. So did I," Cassie said as the three held hands and headed off to find Timmy.